"YOU GIVE ME GREAT HAPPINESS, BUT NEVER HURT."

Li smiled and wriggled out from under him. "I believe I know a way, Long Custis, that will turn a minute into an hour and make you sure that the mountains will crumble before the next daylight. You are will-ing?"

"I expect I would be willing," Longarm said.

"Then please, Long Custis, lie on your back with your eyes closed. Put all thoughts of every kind away from your mind. And allow me the honor of giving you pleasure."

Longarm grinned and did as he was asked.

TABOR EVANS

LONGARM

AND THE
BOUNTY HUNTERS

A JOVE BOOK

LONGARM AND THE BOUNTY HUNTERS

A Jove Book / published by arrangement with
the author

PRINTING HISTORY
Jove edition / August 1983

ISBN: 0-515-06258-8

Jove books are published by The Berkley Publishing Group,
200 Madison Avenue, New York, N.Y. 10016. The words
"A JOVE BOOK" and the "J" with sunburst are trademarks
belonging to Jove Publications, Inc.

PRINTED IN THE UNITED STATES OF AMERICA

Chapter 1

The woman was pretty enough to deserve a second look. Or a third or a fourth, for that matter. The face beneath her fashionable bonnet was young and lovely, yet the halo of hair rimming her attractive features was almost pure white, with just the faintest tinge of gold to hint of color. He could not be sure of her figure, swathed as she was in a cloak, but imagination would suffice where nature was not on display.

Longarm could not avoid letting a slight smile tug at his lips as he tipped his hat to the passing lady. He was flattered to catch a furtive, sideways glance of her eyes toward his as she passed him on the Colfax Avenue sidewalk.

When she was well out of sight and hearing, he permitted himself a sigh and a smile. Not that he had any illusions about himself. Tall, lean-hipped, and broad-shouldered, his tanned features were more ruggedly masculine than truly handsome. And in his brown tweed suit he was hardly in a class with the dandies who surely

1

flocked around a lady of such beauty and obvious breeding.

Still, a man can always entertain pleasant thoughts, so long as he confines them to their proper place. The pale-haired woman certainly had brightened his day.

He turned into the entrance of the Federal Building and made his way by long habit to the United States Marshal's office, hoping as he did so that Billy Vail was not going to ruin his pleasant mood with anything so distracting as work. A few more days to idle the time away over on Larimer Street would be just fine with him.

Impulsively, Longarm flipped his flat-crowned Stetson toward the standing coat rack as he entered the office and had the additional satisfaction of pegging the brown hat with a "ringer" square on top of the rack. He was whistling when he let himself into Vail's inner office.

"Nothing big on at the moment so I'm to make myself useful by looking for low-lifes over in the tenderloin, right, Billy?" He turned and started back out the door without waiting for an answer.

"Whoa!"

Longarm snapped his fingers in mock disgust, but he did stop and turn around. "Shucks."

Billy Vail's round, pink face split into a grin. "It was worth the try, I suppose." He motioned toward a straight-backed wooden chair. "Make yourself comfortable."

Longarm sighed and sat. "I hope you can promise me one thing, at the very least," he said.

Vail's right eyebrow hiked upward toward his shiny, bald pate.

"At least tell me you have something useful for me to do, instead of wet-nursing some damn prisoner halfway across the country or burying me in a pile of moldy old records somewhere." He patted his chest and coughed. "Dust is bad for the lungs, you know."

The chief marshal looked solemn. "I'm sorry to hear you say that. A records search is exactly what I had in mind for you." He pursed his lips and tented his fingers, peering inside his hands as if to ponder the situation.

"But it wouldn't do for me to ignore the health of a deputy," he went on. "Wouldn't do at all. Lung problems, was that it?"

Longarm refused to answer. It seemed he had playfully opened his mouth. Now Billy Vail was about to fill it.

"Yes. Well, that settles it, Longarm. Wouldn't do for me to aggravate your lung problems. And I have heard that traveling in the mountains is very good for the correction of such difficulties. I definitely think you should take a trip into the mountains."

"Did you have any particular place in mind?"

"Now that you ask, I just might have." Billy straightened in his chair and leaned forward over his desk. He fingered a small pile of papers there. This time he looked genuinely serious. The joking, Longarm concluded, was over. "Do you remember a series of train robberies not long ago?"

"Of course," Longarm said. "Two of them, if I remember correctly. One on the Colorado Central. Another on the Denver and Rio Grande. Both cleared up and off the books, as I recall."

Billy grunted. "So it seems. All guilty parties brought to justice." He waved his hand in dismissal of the fact, or perhaps in disregard for the local authorities who had done the cleaning up and the book-clearing.

"You don't think so?" Longarm asked, surprised.

"The evidence is irrefutable," Billy said. "Or so they claim. That, frankly, remains to be seen. Also irrefutable is the fact that another or a similar gang seems to have taken up where those earlier gentlemen—now deceased, I might add—left off."

"Are we involved this time?" Despite a theoretical attitude of mutual cooperation between local authorities and federal officers, Deputy Marshal Custis Long knew

3

all too well that theory and practice quite often travel different roads. Local people, even state agencies, could be sensitive about their jurisdictions, and a federal officer had to be particular about whose laws he was enforcing.

Billy smiled. "No question about it. Both of those other gangs were *very* careful about the cars they entered during their robberies. Avoided even *looking* at a mail car. That's what makes me so suspicious about this new outbreak. Once again the train robbers have made it a point to avoid breaking into the mail cars.

"But this time they were unlucky. Two days ago they hit a train on the Denver, South Park and Pacific. At the time of the robbery the postal clerk had gone forward to have a word with the conductor. Just bad luck, actually; in any event, the fellow was somewhat braver than he was smart. He fired at them and they returned the fire. They shot straighter than he did. So now we have a federal violation. Deadly assault on a federal officer in the commission of his duties."

"Hard luck."

"For the postal clerk *and* for the train robbers," Vail agreed.

"Do we have a starting place?" Longarm asked.

Billy gave him a canary-eating smile. "Better than that. We have one of the robbers. The dead clerk wasn't totally inefficient. He managed to wound one of them. That gentleman is now in custody in the Park County jail in Fairplay. I have an idea he might have some interesting things to say."

"I'm a pretty fair listener," Longarm said.

"The thin air will do your lungs a world of good," Billy told him.

Chapter 2

The narrow-gauge cars of the Denver, South Park and Pacific were hardly substantial enough to entice robbers. Most of the train was devoted to freight. Ore cars being hauled back empty, a flatbed carrying several monstrously huge pieces of equipment Longarm could not identify, a few closed freight cars, and a single passenger coach that was placed entirely too close to the engine for comfort. Soot and cinders came in through the open windows frequently, but the choice seemed to be that or suffocation.

Longarm had chosen his seat with extraordinary care. The upholstery of most of them was heavily patterned with stains of a nature Longarm decided he would rather not know. Most of the passengers were in the late stages of benders, obviously mine workers on their way home from blowouts in Denver.

Worse still, all of the other occupants of the grubby car were male. Longarm liked male companionship as well as the next fellow, but enough was enough. He slumped dourly against the wood of the side wall and smoked one cheroot after another.

After some hours of a grindingly slow uphill climb, the conductor appeared from wherever he had been lurking to the rear of the passenger coach. He strutted officiously to the front of the coach and made a two-minute production of consulting with his watch before he spoke. "Como. Next stop, Como. Twenty-five-minute stop at Como for those as wants to stretch. Next stop, Como." He snapped the face of his watch closed and marched back to the rear of the coach and beyond.

Longarm sighed. His fine mood of the previous morning was gone. He hoped it would come again some day.

He could hear the grind and squeal as the brakemen set their wheels and the train began to slow. At least the stop would break the monotony. He was feeling too low to enjoy the spectacular scenery the train had been passing through.

The DSP&P train came to a clanking, jolting halt, and behind them the conductor called, "Como. All out for Como."

But damn, Longarm thought, *what's the name of this place?* He joined the flow of passengers out of the coach, all of them moving with the stiff-legged, awkward gait of men who have sat too long. Longarm yawned.

"Hey! Where the hell—" The train was backing away from the platform. Longarm had visions of being left adrift with his luggage one place and his transportation-less self elsewhere.

"It's all right," someone beside him said. "They're picking up coal cars an' dropping the empty buckets."

"Oh." Longarm smoothed his mustache the way a bird would smooth its ruffled feathers. It did not particularly please him to see that his finger came away grimed with coal soot. He felt as if the inside of his nose was caked with the stuff.

"There's a stand over here selling coffee if you want

6

some," the man beside him said.

Longarm smiled. "You lead and I'll buy."

Longarm glanced at the man, paying attention this time. The fellow was nearly as tall as Longarm and was much more handsome in a silver-haired, distinguished way. His suit was perfectly cut and made of the finest cloth. The stone in his stickpin would have represented a year's wages for a hardrock miner.

As brief as Longarm's trained inspection had been, the man noticed and correctly interpreted it. "No calluses," he said with a warm smile. He stopped and turned to face Longarm, holding his hand forward. "I'm Brent MacRae, partner in the Little Mac Mine and Mill. And you are?"

Longarm shook. "Custis Long."

MacRae looked him up and down, making no pretense about it. Longarm's tweed suit, matching vest, and linen shirt were presentable, serviceable, and ordinary. "Geologist?" MacRae speculated. "Or an engineer, perhaps?"

Longarm laughed. "Civil servant," he said. He was not much given to lying—and he was not really telling an untruth—but quite a few honest people felt uncomfortable in the presence of a peace officer. Consideration for MacRae's comfort was the reason Longarm answered as he did.

"Pity," MacRae said. "There's intelligence in your eyes. If you were a mining man looking for work, you'd have been hired by now."

Longarm found himself liking MacRae. With decision makers like this self-assured man in it, the high mining country obviously was not all muck and beer.

"Come along, Mr. MacRae. I believe I owe you a cup of railroad coffee."

"Boiled soot is more like it, but it could be worse."

They lined up behind a fast-talking, hand-waving group of working men who were speaking a language Longarm could not even identify, much less understand. When the working men had gone and their own two cups were being served, MacRae said, "Italians. There's quite a colony of them working in the coal mines down here."

"*Down* here?" Longarm asked. "If the air gets any thinner, I might have to have a bag of Denver air shipped up just so I can sleep at night."

MacRae laughed. "We're still practically in the lowlands, Mr. Long. You'll get used to it, of course. In the meantime, don't do any running or take any stairs too fast."

"I'll try to remember that."

They barely had time to finish the near-boiling coffee before the train had been remade and returned to the platform. It seemed natural for Longarm and MacRae to sit together for the rest of the journey, slower still now with the added weight of the coal cars, even if most of the serious climbing had already been done, and the ride was more pleasant with company.

The train pulled over Red Hill Pass and rolled through the small station there without stopping.

"Poor planning," MacRae observed as the tiny station slipped behind them.

"What?"

"Poor planning, I said. Fairplay is the business center of the district here. It's right over there, about four miles away." He pointed in a generally westerly direction. "But all the road traffic runs through Garo, south of here. That's where I'll be getting off. It makes for a longer drive, that's all."

Longarm nodded.

A moment later the conductor was back, displaying his watch and feeling important. "Garo next stop, Garo. All off for Fairplay, Alma, Mosquito Gulch, and points beyond. Next stop Garo."

"Reckon this is my stop too, then," Longarm said. "I expect they have stage service over to Fairplay?"

8

"Hell, Custis, if that's where you're going, allow me to drive you. My home if on the far edge of Fairplay, so I have to go right through town regardless, and I wired ahead for a carriage to meet me. You're more than welcome to ride along."

Longarm thanked him and accepted.

They made the drive from the railroad to Fairplay in less than an hour, and MacRae dropped Longarm off at the best of the town's several hotels and boarding houses, with a reminder that Longarm should "come visit sometime." Longarm promised that he would.

"Enjoy your stay in the district, Custis."

"Thank you, Brent. Take care now."

Longarm picked up his bags and mounted the steps to the hotel lobby. Before he got carried away with socializing, he reminded himself, there was a little matter of some work that needed doing.

By the time he checked into the hotel it was too late to expect to find the sheriff at work, and unless there was good reason to the contrary Longarm generally found it better to go through the formalities with the properly elected official or political appointee. Deputies in rural areas frequently tended to lack initiative as well as authority.

Longarm made himself comfortable in the small but reasonably clean room he had been given and made sure he would be able to find the lamp table and matches if he should return to the unfamiliar room after dark. He had no reason for concern that he knew about, but habitual caution made him pluck a few hairs from the back of his neck and place them on drawer edges and across the openings of his bags. A man never knew when such a habit would pay off. He was not particularly hungry, so he took a turn around the town before dinner.

The courthouse, a tall and narrow stone building, was a block off the main street. The jail was on the top floor of the courthouse. Longarm stopped to look at the struc-

9

ture but did not go inside. His man would be there in the morning, too.

Most of the buildings in town, unlike the courthouse, were built of squared logs, although from looking at the surrounding countryside now it would be hard to guess where all those logs might have come from. As with most mining camps, the land around Fairplay had been stripped of timber for buildings and for mine tunnel shores. There was no immediate evidence of mining activity in Fairplay except for a few placer operations in the South Platte headwaters running beside the town.

The community itself was in the broad, grassy basin known as South Park, surrounded by mountains but itself remaining slightly apart from them. The exercise, even at a walking pace, told him, though, that the altitude was much higher than that of Denver. A few hundred yards left him aware of the thin atmosphere.

He stopped, pulled a slim cheroot from his pocket, and nipped one end from it. *Gets much worse,* he thought, *there won't be enough air to light a damn match.* The match lighted, in spite of his doubts. He cupped his hands around it and bent his head toward it.

"Shit!"

The expletive, coming from somewhere not far to Longarm's left, was followed closely by a high-pitched, singsong burst of chatter that sounded something like a flock of pinyon jays cussing the hell out of a hawk. All that noise seemed to be in a woman's voice, though.

Longarm shook his match out and stepped around the storefront near which he was standing into an alley between the buildings.

There were two men there, roughly dressed and unshaven. And a girl.

The girl's back was to Longarm, but he quickly judged her to be an Indian girl. A spill of jet-black hair hung well below waist level. At the moment the hair was

10

swinging wildly from side to side as she struggled in one man's grasp.

The other man seemed uninterested in the scrap just then. He was doubled over and leaning against the log wall beside him, clutching at his crotch and looking mighty pale. Longarm grinned. The girl was small, but it looked as though she was not completely defenseless. She seemed to have gotten in at least one well-placed kick.

"Need some help, boys?" Longarm asked. His voice was mild, but his normally calm blue eyes had turned the glinty shade of gunmetal.

The man who was holding the girl froze and looked over her head. He seemed surprised but not particularly upset that he had been caught with her there.

"Little bitch took a kick at my partner here. We was figurin' to teach her a lesson. Reckon now it'll be a real *good* lesson."

Longarm took his time about drawing another match from his pocket and lighting his cigar. When it was pulling well, he said, "Kinda small, ain't she? I was always told if their head don't stick out of a barrel they ain't big enough yet."

The man barked out something that might have been a laugh. "She's big enough. Tight, too. Ain't you, Jenny?" He took a firmer grip on her arm with his left hand and reached down to grope her with his right.

"You boys make yourselves kinda free with the little lady's person, don't you?" Longarm observed quietly.

The man gave him a look that was half grin and half leer. "Hell, man, this kind don't count."

The other man was sufficiently recovered from his injury to be able to straighten up. He let go of himself and took a step toward the girl. The slump of her small shoulders seemed to indicate that she had become resigned to her fate. Longarm did not at all like what he saw in the man's eyes.

11

"Boys," he said, "I think we need to have a discussion here about your manners."

The injured man shifted his attention from the immobile girl and directed his fury toward Longarm.

"Butt out, you son of a bitch, or I'll stomp on your head some. *Then* I'll carve me a piece of ol' Jenny."

Longarm sighed. "And I'd got the impression folks around here were sociable." He set his cheroot between his teeth and with his left hand pulled his badge from his coat pocket. He grinned at them, his teeth white against the nearly black stick of the cheroot.

The angry man recoiled, then quickly recovered. He squinted at Longarm. "You ain't no county deppity."

"Federal," Longarm agreed.

The man laughed. "Then you got no right to butt in. So butt out. I'll *still* stomp your ass."

"Boys," Longarm said patiently, "there is something you need to learn. Assaulting a federal officer is a crime. That's the first thing. The other is, I'm a lazy kind of jasper. I got damn small patience with creeps like you. And I sure don't intend to waste my time and energy slugging it out with you." He grinned. "What I'm saying is, I wouldn't even pretend to fight fair."

Longarm scratched his belly. His hand moved a few inches further to the cross-draw holster that rode over his left hip, and the big double-action .44-40 Colt appeared in his fist. "See?"

At last the two men seemed to get the message. The one who had been doing all the threatening went white again.

"I din't. . . . " The man's eyes were wide and staring. "I ain't *armed,* mister." Like most miners, he was not wearing a belly gun.

"I am," Longarm said in a conversational tone of voice. He raised the Colt and sighted down the barrel toward the man's brisket.

As Longarm had been almost certain they would do,

both men turned and began to run down the alley, scattering litter and making quite a racket as they went.

Longarm briefly considered the idea of sending a sizzler past their ears to add to the lesson—assuming they might have learned anything from the experience—but as quickly decided against it. When a man starts to play with firearms he is playing the idiot, and any trouble he gets into is his own damn fault. He put the revolver away.

The girl was still standing in the middle of the alley, where she had been abandoned by her would-be attackers. She stood with her shoulders hunched. Small as she was, Longarm thought, she could not be more than fourteen. He went to her.

"It's all right now, little miss. I—"

She turned to face him for the first time, and Longarm stopped in mid-sentence. Quickly, the impulse coming unbidden, he reached up and snatched off his Stetson. "Excuse me, ma'am."

The woman smiled at him.

Expecting a very young Indian girl, Longarm was confronted instead by a tiny but quite mature Chinese woman.

Her eyes were obsidian almonds in a golden-hued face that was exquisitely formed. She was dignified more than actually beautiful, but that dignity was more than enough to set her above the common run of womankind.

Fourteen? Shallow traces of wrinkles around her eyes and at the corners of her mouth lent character to her face rather than taking anything away from it. But she could have been anywhere from twenty-five to forty-five. Longarm could not begin to judge her age now that he had a clear look at her.

Her figure, what he could judge of it beneath the simple, straight-falling garment she wore, was approximately correct for an Occidental fourteen-year-old girl. She could not have stood five feet tall, and probably missed that mark by several inches.

The woman smiled at him. "Thank you for helping me." There was a light, lilting quality to her voice, but her grammar and accent were quite correct.

"You're more than welcome, ma'am." He replaced his hat and tapped the ash from the end of his cheroot. He was still feeling a bit flustered by the surprise of seeing her when he had expected much...He thought about it. Much *less* was what he had been expecting.

"You saved me a great deal of pain and the price of a new shift. I am grateful." Damned if she didn't put her hands together and bow.

Longarm bowed back to her. He had almost forgotten that habit.

"You are a federal officer?" she asked.

"Yes, ma'am." He introduced himself. "Most folks call me Longarm. I'd be pleased if you would too."

"If that would please you, of course I shall." She smiled. "Longarm."

"Yes, ma'am. Well, I'd better get along and find myself some supper. I don't think those two will bother you again."

Her face had been perfectly composed in spite of the ordeal she had just experienced, but now a change flickered briefly across her features, tightening her forehead. As quickly as it had come it was gone.

"What is it?" Longarm asked.

"It is nothing. Excuse me." She bowed again and would have gone, but he stopped her.

"Please."

She shrugged. "Those men or others—it hardly matters. A yellow Celestial is not human, eh?" She smiled, bitterly this time. "I told you it was nothing. As I am nothing."

"Whoa, now! Whatever gave you that idea?"

"Experience, Longarm. Much experience. Please, now, I...No, I have an idea. If it would not be beneath you to accept from so lowly a person as I."

14

"I don't know what you have in mind, but I wish you'd quit this humble nonsense." He glared down the alley in the direction the two miners had taken. "Why, you have more class and more humanity in one small finger than a whole pack of that kind ever will. And if you have all that much experience, you probably know that not all of us are like that scummy pair."

"Yes. Those experiences have been few, but I acknowledge them. I apologize. I did not mean to categorize you with their type. Please accept my apology."

"No apology necessary. Now, what was this idea of your?"

"You are hungry and I am grateful. I would consider it a privilege if you would allow me to prepare and serve your meal." She bowed very low.

Longarm had been looking forward to a thick, tallow-fried steak, fried potatoes, and rich gravy. He had an idea that would not exactly be what he could expect at a Chinese table. Still, there did not seem to be any way he could gracefully refuse. Not after coming across as so open-minded and liberal. Refuse now and she would damn sure take it as an indication that he considered her home and her cooking beneath him.

"I'd be honored, ma'am," he told her with a smile.

Chapter 3

"Very good, ma'am." *Sort of,* he amended to himself. Whatever it was, it did not threaten to replace good old American beef and potatoes. The dish was a mixture of meat chunks and vegetables, most of which he did not recognize, in a thin sauce. The meat was pork. At least, he thought it was pork. In fact, he *hoped* it was pork. He did not quite have enough nerve to inquire.

"Thank you." She poured more tea for him. The woman had been hovering by his side throughout the entire meal. Twice he had asked her to join him; both times she'd refused. A custom of some sort, he'd concluded finally, and let it drop. For sure he could not complain about the service. Every need was met and most were anticipated. The woman gave him the slightly uncomfortable sensation of having a personal body servant. It was an odd feeling for Custis Long.

Longarm emptied his plate and pushed it back. It was whisked away as soon as his hand left it. He pulled out a cheroot and was greeted immediately by a lighted straw

17

held beneath the tip of the cigar. The woman bowed to him.

"Won't you sit with me now?"

She smiled and sat. By then it came as a surprise. And left him with the problem of conversation.

"I believe those—uh—men said your name is Jenny?"

Again there was that faint flicker that might have been the beginnings of a frown, quickly wiped away.

"It isn't Jenny," he said, this time not really as a question.

"No," she said. "My name is Chen Li. The nearest familiar name seems to be Jenny. Therefore I am now known as Jenny."

"May I call you Chen?"

She giggled. It was the first genuinely happy sound he had heard her make, and the expression that went with it very nearly made her look young enough to match her small size.

"Did I say something funny?"

"No. Please excuse me. I am aware of your customs. I should not have laughed. Pardon me. It is that our names are, from yours, backward. My given name is Li. It is as if you were known as Long Custis. But please call me what you would wish. Chen or Jenny or Li— whichever is comfortable to your tongue."

"All right, Li."

"Thank you. No Occidental has ever called me by my given name before. It is a kindness."

"You're a kind lady." He inhaled a pleasant draw on his cheroot and took a swallow of the tea, not quite so good now that it was cooling. "Tell me about yourself. How did you manage to come to a place as remote as this?"

Li shrugged. "It is a very simple thing. I was married. My husband came to this country years ago to work on the railroad. I joined him five years ago. He was then working on another railroad. And then another. Last year

18

he was working on the South Park. There was an accident." She gave him a wan smile. "Now I do that which is expected of me. I take in laundry. I raise and sell what vegetables I can. I act as a scapegoat. Is that word correct, please?"

"I'm afraid so."

"But again I must apologize. I should not forget myself so. I have a very easy life here, for a Chinese. Across the mountain there in Leadville they have a law which says no Chinese may remain in their city overnight. Here I am allowed the nights as well as the days. I am fortunate."

"No, but you are generous. You're entitled to some hate, I'd guess, but if you feel any you do a good job of not showing it. My opinion would be that the town is fortunate to have you for a citizen, Li."

"You are much too kind."

Much more of this, Longarm decided, and it would turn into a flatter-flinging contest. He pushed his chair back from the table in the immaculately clean shanty that was Li's home.

"I've taken up too much of your evening," he said. "You'll want to eat and get some rest."

"No. Please." She came quickly to her feet, and there was a look of real pleading in her eyes.

"Are you all right, Li?"

"Of course." But he thought he could see a welling of glistening tears in those almond-shaped eyes.

"What is it?"

"I am being impertinent. I should remember my place." There was definitely a tear in the corner of her eye now.

"Please."

"It has been so very long since I was able to speak with anyone who might be considered . . ." She shook her head unhappily from side to side. "No, I must not assume too much."

"A friend?" Longarm prompted.

19

The simple word was too much for her. She was openly weeping now. She bit into her trembling underlip, but she nodded.

Without thinking about it, meaning only to comfort, Longarm moved quickly to her side and wrapped his arms around her. He crooned to her soothingly without words.

Her sobs became stronger, her thin shoulders shuddering. She was so tiny that her face was buried only a little bit higher than his belly, and he could feel the heat of her tears through the cloth of his shirt.

After a time the sobbing subsided. He reached down and with his fingertips tilted her head back. Her eyes were puffy from the tears, and her face was flushed.

"I'd be real proud to call you a friend," he said softly, "and prouder yet if you would call me one."

Li wrapped her arms around his waist and held onto him very tightly for several minutes.

He felt more than heard her take a deep breath. This time when she looked up at him—it seemed a very long distance, so great was the difference between his height and hers—she was smiling with real pleasure. Longarm wiped away a few lingering tear-tracks from her cheeks. He was not exactly prepared for what she did then.

Li reached up to capture his strong hand in her tiny one. She turned his wrist so that his palm was open and toward her. She pressed her lips against his palm and, incredibly, he could feel the tantalizing flick of her tongue. His reaction was immediate and predictable.

He tried to pull away. "Li, I . . ."

She looked up at him, still holding onto his hand. "Longarm, my friend, I have been married and am now without a husband. I have been . . . made use of . . . by drunken Occidentals more than once. Those two in the alley have taken me before. And others as well. But it has been a very long time since I was able to bring myself to a man as a gift within my power to give. I would give myself to you with joy and with pleasure. If . . ." She blinked and pulled back slightly. "If you want such an unworthy offering." She was not looking him in the eyes now. Longarm guessed that she was afraid he would refuse her.

In answer, Longarm bent and kissed her. With a choked cry of sheer joy, Li surged up into his embrace.

Li giggled. She was still on her knees after helping him off with his drawers. Damned if she had not insisted on acting once again as a body servant would, undressing him and hanging his clothes with great care. He was finally naked now and was faintly embarrassed. He could not help wondering how he compared with a man of another race.

"Something funny?" he asked.

She giggled. "I have had a thought, Longarm. You should have been born to a Chinese name."

"Why?"

"It is simple. To have named you Long Custis would have been most appropriate." She reached up and ran her fingers down the length of his maddeningly erect shaft and cupped his scrotum in her palm. Her touch was so light he could scarcely feel it, which might have had something to do with it's being so damnably effective. "I believe that from now on I shall think of you always as Long Custis."

Longarm groaned.

"Sit, please. No, on the edge of the bed. So—yes." She smiled at him.

Li quickly pulled her shift over her head, and the tattered chemise followed it. She had nothing else on. Kneeling, she leaned back and gave him time to look at her. Longarm swallowed hard.

Tiny. No more than a mouthful anywhere he might look. But small as her body was, its proportions were perfect. She was a woman in miniature. Breasts very

21

small, but high and nicely rounded. Hips swelling out beneath a waist that he might almost have encircled with the fingers of one hand. Hair a gleaming flow. Practically no—he had to look several times to make sure the dim lamplight was not playing tricks on him—practically no pubic hair.

"You're lovely," he said hoarsely, sure she would be having the same questions in her mind that he had had in his. Li looked as pleased as if he had just given her a great gift.

She shuffled forward on her knees to the bedside where Longarm waited. She took his hand in hers again and caressed his palm with the tip of her tongue.

Then, as if it were the most natural thing in the world, she guided his hand to the back of her head and gave her attention to his penis. At first the soft touches of tongue and lips were so light that they were barely felt. Gradually they became bolder. Longarm was about to explode.

"Careful, I . . ."

"It is all right, my long friend. Here first to take away the urgency. Then again so that we both may enjoy it."

Longarm lay back on the scratchy ticking of her cot and let the sensations sweep over and through him. She still was touching him more lightly and delicately than he had ever felt before. Logically, a light touch should have given little. Improbably, the pinnacle he was building toward was awesomely high.

He reached the crest and flowed outward in a slow, smooth outpouring that lasted three forevers. It seemed he would never stop. A strangely gentle flood of heat pulsed out of his loins. She stayed with him throughout, holding him in her mouth and ministering to him with her fingertips until he was totally spent.

Longarm felt drained, literally and figuratively. If a pack of toughs on the wanted lists had chosen that moment to break into the shanty and horsewhip him, Long-

22

arm was sure he would not have been able to raise a finger to defend himself.

With a struggle he managed to sit back up. "That was . . . *powerful*. You took it all, Li. There's nothing left."

She laughed and came to her feet. The smooth, hairless mound of her vee was just below eye level, the dark-tipped swell of her breasts just above his eyes. He reached out to stroke that small, wondrous body. Her flesh was cool satin.

"I think you are wrong, Long Custis." She guided his hand to her mound and smiled at his expression. Then she lay beside him and invited him to enter, a mouthful of woman with the body of a child and the talents of a courtesan.

Longarm was indeed wrong. He was not nearly so drained as he had thought.

Chapter 4

The sheriff was a small man wearing sleeve garters and an unbuttoned vest. His coat and a derby hat were hanging on a rack nearby. He leaned back in a swivel chair and propped his feet on his desk, lacing his hands behind his neck. "Deputy, huh? We don't see many of you federal boys up here."

"Well, I expect to be around for a while. Until I get this job done anyway," Longarm said.

"Might not be very long, then."

"Is that a vote of confidence, Sheriff?"

The man snorted. "Not hardly. Far as I can tell, you boys ain't any better than anybody else, 'cept for being overpaid in comparison with my deputies. At least my people know the country. I don't reckon you can make that claim."

"I can't claim to know the country well, no. Can't claim to be overpaid either," Longarm said mildly.

The sheriff chose to ignore that. "Anyway, the railroad's put up a bounty on the fellas that has been robbing

25

them. I figure some Yankee dollars will do the job that a damn-Yankee deputy marshal likely *can't* do."

That rather clearly explained the sheriff's feelings toward the federal government, Longarm thought. As far as he himself was concerned, the War was long since over. But not everyone felt the same way.

He was used to dealing with that, though. The bad news was about that bounty.

A posted bounty drew bounty hunters in very much the same way a pile of crap in the woods drew flies. Longarm's opinion was that he preferred the flies to the bounty hunters. Had more respect for them, too.

A dead-or-alive bounty was virtually the same as an outright request that the wanted man be brought in dead, for damned few bounty hunters would go to the trouble necessary to bring in a live prisoner. The way Longarm read the Constitution, a man was deemed innocent until or unless a court of law proved him otherwise. He saw nothing there that gave a railroad or a bank the right to issue an execution warrant before that man was convicted.

On the other hand, no one was asking his interpretation on that subject, and the law clearly allowed both bounties and bounty hunters. It was just something he had to get along with, like it or not.

He sighed and pulled a cheroot from his pocket.

"I'd ruther you didn't light up in here, Deputy," the sheriff said. He was giving Longarm a rather nasty smile when he said it, and for a moment Longarm could not think why. Then he realized. There was an overflowing ashtray on the sheriff's desk.

Petty son of a bitch, Longarm thought. He put the cheroot back into his pocket unlighted.

"I take it we can continue to count on your official cooperation, Sheriff?" he asked.

The sheriff was still smiling. "Of course you can. My official cooperation will be duly given."

Longarm smiled back at him. "Of course." He stood up, but did not offer to shake hands. "I assume, then, that I can interview the prisoner now?"

"Ayuh, if you intend to do that at all I expect you'd best do it today. The little prick hangs tomorrow."

That took Longarm by surprise. "You hadn't said anything about that before."

"I don't recall you asked me."

Longarm bit back the reply he wanted to make and observed, "You have quick justice around here, Sheriff."

"It don't take us long to do the right thing, and that's a fact. No question the little son of a bitch is guilty. So why should the good people up here pay to feed him any longer'n need be?"

"That's an interesting way to look at it. Now, if I could see him . . . ?"

Without rising, the sheriff turned his head and bellowed, "Lem!"

The office door opened and a hairy jailer, presumably Lem, stuck his head in.

"Take this bluebelly deppity up to have a talk with our guest. Let 'im stay as long as he likes." The sheriff chuckled. "Can't have anybody saying we din't cooperate, can we?"

The jailer seemed just about as friendly as the sheriff, so Longarm kept his mouth shut as he was shown into the only occupied cell on the courthouse top floor.

The prisoner looked frightened when Longarm and the jailer entered the cellblock.

"I ain't gonna unlock for you," Lem said. "No need for it, an' we don't want to take no chances on losin' him." He laughed. "Not till tomorra, anyhow."

Longarm said nothing until Lem was out of hearing.

He looked around the bare hallway, but there was nothing for him to sit on. With a shrug he pulled the cheroot from his pocket again, lighted it, and tossed the spent match onto the floor. With any luck, Lem would be angry when he saw a mess on his floor.

The prisoner was sitting on the edge of his bunk eyeing Longarm with a wary glance. He still looked nervous. Longarm introduced himself.

"You aren't bulling me?" the prisoner asked.

"Why should I do that?"

"You don't want to haul me outa here?"

"Of course not." Longarm was genuinely puzzled.

The boy relaxed. He was barely old enough to shave, and the pallor of fear made him look even younger. He apparently had been something of a dandy before his arrest, and Longarm guessed that he likely was fairly new to the "wild West" and had fallen quickly into bad company, thinking it was the tough and rough and ready thing to do.

He had been wounded in the torso and so was wearing only heavy strips of bandages above the waist, but his boots and trousers gave Longarm enough of a clue.

His pants were brown corduroy cut so tight they must have been hellishly uncomfortable to wear and decorated—certainly it was not for utilitarian purposes, as any trousers that tight could not possibly fall down—with a wide belt and a huge buckle of turquoise and German silver. The trousers were tucked into a pair of ornately stitched Texas-style boots that came up nearly knee-high, with tall riding heels that would make them sheer misery to walk in for any distance farther than the wearer could spit. Both trousers and boots looked new, nearly unsullied by dust or wear.

Longarm shook his head. "What's your name, boy?" His name had not been on the wire yet when Longarm left Denver.

"Tristam Gay, sir." He tried to laugh, but it came out as more of a choking sound. "Not a very damn gay sight now, am I?"

"No. I expect you have found yourself all the trouble a body could want."

"Yes, sir." The boy certainly was no smart-ass punk about it, Longarm thought. Reality had boiled away all bravado by now.

"Why were you so frightened when I came in here, Tris? Do you mind if I call you Tris?"

"I don't mind, sir." He took a deep breath and shuddered. "That jailer there, Mr. Lemuel..."

"*Mr.* Lem? It sounds strange to hear you call him that."

"That's what he told me to call him, sir. Anyway, he was telling me that a couple of years ago they had a fellow in this very same jail an' the judge was going to let him off, so the folks in town come up and tied a rope to those bars right over there and the other end to this fellow's neck, and they threw him out the window, sir. Mr. Lemuel said there was talk they might do the same to me, even though the court said I have to hang for being with that crowd when they shot that mail clerk. Mr. Lemuel said there was a bunch of talk like that." He shuddered again.

They were really going easy on the kid, Longarm saw. Next they would probably allow him to keep a few pets in his cell. Like maybe throw a bucketful of rattlesnakes in for him.

"Bad luck there was a district court in session at the time," Longarm said.

"Oh, it wasn't no district court, sir. They brought me up before the justice of the peace here." .

Longarm nodded. Somehow he was not particularly surprised. Still, while he was no expert on state law, the trial would probably stand up. Hell, it had to. In a matter of hours there would be no one around to file an appeal.

"You did do it, didn't you, Tris?"

"Yes, sir, I done it all right. I don't mean that I shot anybody. I've never done that—ever. But I was with them just the same. The prosecutor said being with them was the same as doing it. Is that right, sir?"

"It sure is, Tris. In the eyes of the law, you are as guilty as the man who pulled the trigger. He was telling you the truth."

"I kind of figured he was. He didn't seem like a bad sort." The boy sighed. "I sure messed up, didn't I?"

"It would be fair to say that you did, son." Longarm stood for some time pulling at his cigar and happily tapping the ashes onto the cellblock floor. "I might be able to help you, Tris."

"Yes, sir?"

"What I want you to do, Tris, is to give me the names of the other men involved in this robbery. Then I may be able to help you."

"Oh, I couldn't do that, sir."

"No?"

"No, sir. That's part of the code, you see. A man never welshes on a bet nor tells on his friends. I've always heard that, sir."

"I see." Longarm puffed on his cheroot some more. "Code, huh?"

"Yes, sir."

"Does the code say that it's all right for them to get you hanged when you didn't shoot anybody?"

"I wouldn't know how to answer that, sir."

"Reckon I wouldn't either, if I was in your shoes." Longarm went back to his smoke.

"You really could help me, sir?"

"Uh-huh." He dropped the cheroot onto the floor and ground it out under the toe of his boot. It made a quite satisfactory mess.

"How could that be? I mean, I'm not saying I could do what you want. But if I did...?"

"The way it would work, Tris, would be that you would give me those names. Then I'd go arrest them and take them down to Denver to stand trial in the Federal District Court. Shooting a postal clerk is a federal offense, you see."

"Yes, sir, I remember being told something about that."

"Right. Well, the thing is, if I carry someone down to stand trial, there has to be a witness against him." He smiled. "Judges won't take my say-so on who ought to go to jail and who shouldn't."

"Yes, sir. They had witnesses against me too."

"Exactly. And since, the way I understand it, all you boys were masked at the time of the holdup, the only one who could stand witness would be you, Tris. And if I expect you to stand witness, I'll have to make sure you're alive to do it. Then you would have to stand trial yourself again, but I'd tell the judge you were a cooperative witness and helped to convict the rest of the gang.

"Mind now, I'm not offering to let you off scot free. You would have to serve time in prison. Probably twenty years, maybe with time off for good behavior, though that would be up to you afterward. I can't even promise for sure that the sentence would be twenty years. That would be up to the judge to decide.

"But, Tris, I could promise you that you wouldn't hang."

The boy bit his lip and looked away. He thought about it for some time. When he looked back toward Longarm, he asked, "You're sure about that?"

"Uh-huh. I'm sure." Longarm gave him time to ponder it.

"You could for *sure* keep me from hanging?"

"I'd have to send a wire down to my boss in Denver. That means you couldn't take any too long to give me your answer, because then Marshal Vail has to find a judge—a federal judge, not some local J.P.—to issue the proper writs. Then he would wire me back, and I'd take custody of you. I'd put you in cuffs and take you down to Denver. You'd wait for the trials in jail there."

"Down in Denver? Away from here and that damned Lem?"

Longarm noticed that it was no longer "Mr. Lemuel."

"That's right, Tris."

The boy grinned. "Would you happen to have a piece of paper and a pencil on you, sir?"

"I can get one quick enough." He started toward the door, then stopped and turned back. "One more thing, Tris."

"Yes, sir?"

"It probably would be a good idea if neither one of us mentioned this to anyone else until I have that writ and can take you out of here." He smiled. "You more than likely don't want to have any visitors from the town while we're waiting."

Tris grinned. "No, sir, I won't say a word to nobody."

"I'll see you this afternoon, then."

"You son of a bitch." The sheriff's face was mottled red and purple from his anger.

"Careful, now. It wouldn't do for you to have a stroke when you still have most of a year in office yet to serve." Longarm was unperturbed by the sheriff's impotent fury. If anything, he accepted it as a compliment, considering the source.

"That little bastard was sentenced to hang, by God, and you got no right . . ."

"I have *every* right, Sheriff, according to the laws of the United States of America. I also have the duty. And if you haven't figured it out by now, maybe I should tell you. I do figure to perform that duty, any way I have to do it."

"Are you threatening me, Deputy? Because I'll report you so damn fast . . ."

Longarm reached into his pocket and found one of Billy Vail's cards. He flipped it onto the desk. "There's the place to report me to. Feel free. You won't be getting no virgin. I've been complained about so many times already, I can't keep track of the numbers anymore."

"That's prob'ly the first true thing I've heard you say," the sheriff grumbled.

"Are you going to release my prisoner or not, Sheriff?"

The man leaned over to spit into a tin can on the floor beside his desk. When he straightened up he said, "I got to process him out first. Then you can have him."

"If you don't mind, Sheriff, I will watch the processing." Longarm smiled. "I want him healthy enough to walk to the stage stop, you understand."

The sheriff said nothing, but his glare was murderous.

Longarm went with Lem—he had never yet seen the sheriff move from his chair—and kept an eye on things while Tris Gay was processed out of the county jail. As far as Longarm could tell the procedure was strictly a make-work waste of time.

Fair enough warning, he thought.

The afternoon stage had already departed for Garo by the time Lem and the sheriff were done with their processing. Quite a coincidence, Longarm thought with amusement. The next scheduled stage was not until nine-fifteen that evening, late enough for the area miners to have become liquored up and excitable.

Longarm, with Tris cuffed to his left hand, walked out into the empty plaza surrounding the courthouse. The stage stop was a block south and two blocks east. Longarm headed southwest.

"Stage station's over there," Lem shouted behind him.

"Thanks." Longarm continued in the direction he had been headed.

"Where are we going?" Tris asked.

"The hell out of here," Longarm answered.

"What if there's a mob?"

"I don't know about you, boy, but I'm not wearing any steel plates under my shirt. I can be bushwhacked as easy as the next man. And, given a choice, I'd rather

33

not face any mobs. Which is what we'd have to do if we waited for the next stage out. So what I thought we'd do— Ah, here it is. Climb up on that seat, Tris."

There was a carriage parked in front of a mining supply store, a sleek team of bays in the harness.

"What's this?"

"A buggy, boy. What the hell do you think it is?"

"I mean—"

"Borrowed it from a fellow I met on the train the other day." Longarm unlocked the handcuff bracelet from his own wrist and snapped it around the frame of the carriage, then unhitched the bays and climbed into the seat beside Tris.

"My friend said these horses are fast and ready. I hope he was right." He made contact with their bits and backed them away from the rail, then turned down the street toward Garo.

"Ready, boy?"

"Yes, sir."

"That's more than I can claim, but I reckon we're leaving anyway."

Longarm took the buggy whip out of the stock and cracked it above the bays' ears.

The horses were everything Brent MacRae had promised they would be, and the only thing Longarm saw behind them on the trip to the rails was a boil of red dust.

"I guess it would be too much to ask for the train to be robbed while I was aboard," Longarm observed. They were past Como and making the long slide down to Denver.

"Oh, they wouldn't hit it on the downrun, sir."

"No?"

"No, sir. Bert—he's the top name on your list there—he explained that to us. If there was a train coming downrun, we were to hide and not let ourselves be seen, then rush out and build the blockade to stop the up-bound."

"Why's that?"

Tris gave him a look of disappointment, as if the answer should have been obvious. "Trains going down the mountain, sir, are carrying concentrate. That's stuff too heavy to mess with. The ones coming *up*, though, will be carrying payrolls in gold coin. That's the only thing a miner will take his pay in—gold coin. So you only hit the ones coming up."

"Any other instructions?"

"Yes, sir. Several." Tris shook his head. "One of them was to never, ever, no way touch anything connected with the mails. That one we was told over and over again."

"This Bert sounds like a pretty savvy fellow."

"Oh, it wasn't him doing all the planning, sir."

"No?" Longarm's interest was piqued for sure now. He pulled the list Tris had given him from his pocket. "Which one is it?"

"He isn't on there, sir."

"If you . . ."

"I gave you all the names I know, sir. Every one of them. I'll swear to that. I just don't know the boss's name. I only saw him the once, and then he was wearing a sort of hood over his head. It was an old powder bag turned inside out with holes cut for him to see out. I think—I ain't real certain now—but I *think* Bert knows who he is. I don't know if anyone else does, but I don't for sure."

"How did you get mixed up with this crowd?"

Tris shrugged. "I come out here from Pittsburgh, thinking to make my fortune, be a cowboy, you know."

Longarm nodded. He knew, all right. The country was full of disillusioned youngsters like Tris.

"But I wasn't doing all that great. Then I met Pete in a saloon over in Leadville. Pete's the next name on the list below Bert. Anyway, he said I could pick up some easy money if I had some grit in my craw, and I allowed that I had as much grit as anybody. Next thing I knew, we was robbing a train. Did pretty well from it, so we done it again. That's when I got shot. An' here I am."

"Had the gang been together a while when they took you in with them?"

"Oh, no, sir. Bert was just putting them together. He brought Pete in an' Pete found me. It was pretty much like that for the others too, I guess."

"And this fellow with the hood. Where did he fit in?"

"Like I said, I only seen him that one time. That was right at the beginning. But I think Bert was getting orders from him right along. I got that idea, anyway."

"You never heard any sort of name put to him?"

"No, sir. I'd've wrote it down for you if I had."

Interesting, Longarm thought. As far as he was concerned, that one missing name would be worth more to him than all the rest of the names put together.

Certainly this mysterious man knew what he was doing. Staying away from federal crimes was a touch that Longarm did not particularly like to see. It meant the man was smarter—or, at least, more cunning—than the average yahoo with a gun and a lazy streak. The son of a bitch might not be too easy to bring down.

Longarm leaned over to make sure the cuffs were firmly attached to Tris Gay's wrist at one end and to a coach seat on the other. If the boy could get away with a DSP&P seat without waking Longarm, he was entitled to escape. Longarm tipped his head back and closed his eyes. Someone was sure to kick them off the train when it stopped in Denver.

36

Chapter 5

Longarm was in a thoughtful mood when he returned to Fairplay the following afternoon. Turning Tris Gay over to federal custody had been purely routine, but Billy Vail's information, just in over the wire from some place called Buena Vista, was not.

According to local officials there, an alleged robber of the DSP&P trains had been gunned down in Buena Vista, and a pair of bounty hunters had applied for the reward money from the railroad. The dead man's name had been one of those given to Longarm by Tris Gay. Yet no one but Longarm, Gay, and now Billy Vail had seen the list of names.

Neither Vail nor Longarm liked the idea of bounty hunters in general. In particular, they did not want a bunch of amateurs—a mob or quasi-legal bounty hunters, either one—muddying the waters of their investigation, when the man they both wanted more than any other was the mysterious hooded gentleman. Now that they had the names of the gang members, they would have been content to play a waiting game until that knowledge brought them to the leader of the gang. Bounty hunters could well shove a stick into the spokes of their little red wagon.

"You'll have to get up there and find out some more about this," Vail told his deputy.

"First I have to go back to Fairplay and get my gear. I had to leave it there when I brought Tris down," Longarm said.

"You know you should be ready to travel at all times," Vail said peevishly.

"Damn it, Billy, *you* try to handle a prisoner with one hand, carry luggage with the other, an' still be ready to fight off a bunch of crazy locals." Longarm was feeling just as irritated as the marshal.

"All right, do it your own way. You always do, damn you. Go ahead, then."

They had both been angry when they parted.

Now, after the long train ride to cool off in, Longarm was still concerned, but no longer angry. It would be another day yet before he could continue on the DSP&P route to track's end at Buena Vista. The brief stop at Garo would not permit him to retrieve his gear from the hotel in Fairplay and return before the up-bound train continued on.

MacRae had already sent someone to reclaim the borrowed carriage, so Longarm rode into town in the mud wagon that served as a stage on the short route, jammed in between a pair of loud miners who smelled of stale whiskey and last night's vomit. The ride did nothing to improve his humor.

The stage stopped near the courthouse to let the Fairplay passengers off before continuing on to Alma, Mosquito Gulch, and Leadville. Returning to solid, albeit dusty, earth was something of a relief. Longarm brushed the dust of the short trip from his coat and wished he could as easily brush away the lingering smell of his recent companions. He waited until the stage pulled away and strode off in the direction of his hotel.

"Custis."

He stopped. The voice was coming to him in a hoarse whisper from somewhere to his left. His hand crept toward the butt of the double-action .44 beneath his coat.

"Long Custis." He relaxed. The voice was Li's. "Do not turn, please."

Whatever was going on, Chen Li did not want to be seen talking to him. Longarm covered his abrupt halt by pulling a cheroot from his pocket and fussing over the task of lighting it.

"Be very careful, please. Many of the men here are very angry that your prisoner did not hang today. Those who are drunk enough may wish to do you harm. You understand?"

"Uh-huh," he murmured.

"Your hotel room is known. There is talk of a visit in the night." She paused. "My door will not be locked this night, if you wish to use it. I go now." Li did not wait for an answer. Longarm heard a faint swish that might have been moving cloth, then nothing more.

"Thanks," he muttered, in case he had been mistaken.

Gutsy little woman, he thought. The secrecy had been for *his* protection, not hers; and in a town where the Chinese were fair game to be raped or beaten or used however any so-called "white" man might choose to use them. Chen Li probably did not weigh more than eighty-five pounds, and seventy-five of that had to be heart.

He dropped his burnt-out match in the street and ambled on toward the hotel.

Longarm had time to kill. It was much too early, with several hours of daylight remaining, to head for Li's shanty, if he wanted to protect *her* by not advertising his presence under her roof. And he did not think a saloon would be the proper place to kill the time.

He knew himself too well for that. In the mood he was in, one wrong remark by a belligerent drunk and there could be blood spilled. Longarm was in no humor for a childish fistfight and he did not feel like taking any abuse. So he would be better off to avoid the locals if he possibly could. After all, venting one's spleen with loud noises and gunsmoke was not acceptable behavior for a peace officer.

Still, he had to pass the time somewhere. He gave it some thought, reached a conclusion, and stopped at the hotel bar long enough to buy a bottle of Maryland rye to carry along on his errand.

He also made it a point to ask directions of at least half a dozen sober-looking local residents on his way there. He seriously doubted that anyone in town would be foolish enough to cause a ruckus at Brent MacRae's home. And it seemed perfectly appropriate that he should take a few minutes to thank the man for the help he had given him.

The house was tall and somewhat garishly elegant, the eaves and gables decorated with carved woodwork and a round turret standing proud at the northeast corner to overlook the surrounding mountains and grassy parklands.

Damned impressive, Longarm thought as he mounted freshly painted steps to the broad front porch and tugged at the bellpull. The sound of tiny hammers striking on chimes reached him through the leaded glass in the front door.

The door was opened a moment later, and Longarm stood in stunned silence for several long seconds.

He had been expecting MacRae, or possibly a servant. Instead he was confronted by a slim, lovely woman somewhere in her early thirties. She was dressed simply, with understated good taste, and for jewelry wore only a delicate cameo broach at her throat.

Her eyes widened when she saw the caller, and she too was stunned into silence for what seemed a long time, but could only have been a matter of seconds.

At the same instant, as if by some unspoken command, both Longarm and the woman broke into broad smiles.

"Damn!" Longarm yelped.

"Custis?"

"Jane? Janie Doyle?"

With cries of delight coming from both throats, Longarm took a long step forward. He grabbed the woman around the waist and whirled her into the air. She was laughing and touching his cheek as if to reassure herself that the tall deputy's presence was real.

"Custis? I can't believe this!"

"Janie Doyle. I haven't seen you in— Lordy, it's been . . . five years? It can't be that long."

"It is." Her eyes were bright with pleasure, and she gave him a swift, fierce hug of welcome. Then Longarm held her at arm's length and looked at her with genuine fondness.

He released his hold on her shoulders with one hand long enough to snap his fingers. "Donny. Where's my favorite kid in the whole wide world?" he asked happily.

"Upstairs. Oh, I can't wait to tell him that his Uncle Cuss is here."

Longarm laughed. "You wouldn't believe the ribbing I had to take about that nickname. I'll bet he's grown so I wouldn't hardly know him. Why, he'd be . . ."

"Ten, now. It's hard for me to believe, too. And you *wouldn't* know him. You wait right here, Custis. I'll get Donny and be right . . ."

"What is going on out here?" Brent MacRae's voice was coldly demanding. He stepped out of a doorway wearing a velvet smoking jacket and carrying a tumbler. He was scowling. Then he saw Longarm and his delighted wife, and his expression softened. "Custis? Jane? What . . . ?"

"You aren't any more surprised than we are," Longarm said.

41

"I take it you know my wife?" MacRae asked.

"Your wife?"

"Charlie died four years ago," Jane said softly. "Brent and I were married last fall." She brightened again. "You explain it to Brent, please, Custis. I'll run upstairs and get Donny."

MacRae still looked puzzled.

Longarm was shaking his head in wonder and joy. He walked over to join MacRae. "Charlie Doyle and I were friends from way back," he said. "I stood up with him when he and Jane were married, and I was there when Donny was christened. They moved off to try their luck in San Francisco about five years back, and we kinda lost touch after that."

MacRae smiled. "San Francisco is where I was fortunate enough to meet Jane. What a marvelous coincidence, eh?"

"Marvelous indeed." Longarm gripped MacRae by the shoulder. "And I'm happy for both of you, by God. Jane's a fine woman, and that Donny is some boy. They deserve the best. From everything I've seen and heard, MacRae, you'd fall into that category just fine."

MacRae smiled his thanks. "By God, Custis, I think this deserves a drink of celebration."

Longarm held up the bottle of Maryland rye. "I already had something like that in mind, actually—though not for such an excellent reason."

The evening was a pleasure, old friendship and new, talk that could have lasted for hours. Shortly after dark, when Longarm said he had to go, Jane let Donny give his "uncle"—remembered now, after an uncertain start— a good-night hug and walked Longarm to the door.

"We haven't had nearly enough time to visit. Would you come back to see me in the morning, Custis?"

"I have to get up to Buena Vista tomorrow."

"Please? I really need to talk with someone . . . someone who is an old and a trusted friend. Please?"

There was a pleading in her eyes that went far beyond the reserved tone of her voice.

Longarm took only a moment to consider. There was an early train up-bound and another about noon. If he took the latter there should be no harm done. He smiled. "All right."

"Thank you."

Longarm was whistling when he left the MacRae house. The foul mood he had been in earlier was long forgotten.

The point of Longarm's chin was cushioned in the black sprawl of Chen Li's long, silken hair. She was so tiny that her face came only to his neck even when he was socketed deep into the middle of that small, vibrant body, but she was proof positive that diminutive size did not mean any lack of energy.

She had bucked and pumped half the night away, and now once again in the thin light of the early morning she was wrapped around him like a warm, wet loincloth, accepting his every thrust with a matching lunge of her own, grunting with effort and sighing with pleasure. He felt her body shudder, and she leaped beneath him with a last spasm of release.

Even then she did not release her fiercely tight hold on him with arm and leg alike, and Longarm felt himself build higher and even higher in an intense rush to and beyond the summit of pleasure.

He slammed forward and stiffened, holding himself deep within her while he pumped the hot, sticky fluids of passionate release into Chen Li's body.

Longarm rolled quickly aside before he allowed himself the collapse of satiation, afraid of what his much greater weight might do to that small body.

"Damn," he muttered. He was exhausted. He had not been awake more than three quarters of an hour, and already he was exhausted.

He felt Chen Li stir beside him and insinuate herself under his arm to cuddle against his side. Her hand trailed across his chest and down the hard, flat planes of his belly. She stirred again, and he could feel her tongue flickering where her fingertips had just traveled.

Longarm shook his head. "Good grief, woman, no more."

"You are sure?" She was smiling.

"Positive."

"I would make a bet with you."

Longarm grinned at her. "You'd win it too, I reckon, but that isn't the point." He inclined his chin toward the window, covered with greased paper, through which the light was showing stronger now. "It's getting late."

"I understand." Li slipped out of the bed they had shared through the long, pleasant night, unmindful of her nudity, and began to gather up his clothes. She looked quite lovely in the soft play of light and shadow within the shack, and for a moment Longarm regretted that he had to leave.

No doubt about it, she certainly would have won if he had been foolish enough to lay a wager with her about his continued capabilities.

He dressed quickly and checked his Ingersoll before he tucked it into the pocket of his vest. A quarter to seven. He took another look at Li and wondered if he had been a little hasty in deciding it was time to go. Still, he was dressed now, and he wanted to stop for breakfast before he kept his promise to Jane MacRae. He shrugged into his coat and picked Li up to kiss her long and lingeringly before he set her down again.

It was his intention to thank her for her concern and kindness—and certain other attentions as well—but damned if the woman did not bow low toward him and thank *him* before he could get the words out.

Longarm was taken aback for a moment. Then he returned her bow, feeling perhaps a little less foolish than

44

he thought he would, said some polite thank-yous, and stepped out into the morning light. It was much brighter outside. He was feeling, actually, quite good, in spite of thinking he was so exhausted just a few minutes earlier.

The day clerk at the hotel gave him a sharply questioning look when Longarm entered the lobby from the street, but the man said nothing and quickly looked down toward his ledgers.

"Have my bags brought downstairs, would you?" Longarm asked jauntily.

The man might well have been wondering why Longarm had bothered to take the room if he never intended to use it, just as Longarm was wondering what might have taken place in the hotel overnight, but neither man voiced his question.

"Yes, sir, Deputy," the clerk said.

Longarm went into the adjoining saloon/dining hall, tilted a chair back against the wall, and settled into it with a sense of deep contentment. *Not bad work when a fella can find it,* he was thinking.

"Flannel cakes an' pork chops?" the waiter asked. "That's our regular."

Longarm shook his head. He was damned hungry. "Beefsteak," he ordered, "fried in tallow, good and crusty. And fry up some potatoes, too. That and about a gallon of coffee."

The waiter nodded and went away. Longarm grinned and waved to a pair of men at another table. One of the men seemed to go a little pale.

Fancy that, Longarm thought. *Must've had a busy night.*

Not that he cared. He was content with the world.

"Son of a bitch," Longarm said. He was white and trembling with anger. "Excuse me, Janie, I shouldn't have said that."

Jane MacRae said nothing. Her shoulders were shaking with the force of her sobbing. Brent MacRae was at his mine office, and Donny had been sent down to the South Platte with a fishing pole and a friend. The two of them were alone in her kitchen with cold cups of coffee ignored on the table before them.

"I wouldn't..." She gulped, got control of herself, and tried again. "I wouldn't mind if it was just me, Custis. Really I wouldn't. It's a woman's place to provide for her man, whatever it is he needs. I know that. But Donny..." Jane's face twisted and she began to cry again.

"He's a good boy," Longarm said darkly.

"You should...you should..." Her shoulders heaved and she had to stop for a moment. "You should see the welts on his back and his bottom. I just...I just don't know what to *do*, Custis."

"I do." Longarm's voice was soft, but there was the menace of cold steel in it.

"No," Jane said quickly. "You mustn't say anything to him, Custis. For our sakes. Please. For Donny's and mine. You just don't know. It would be...awful. After you were gone."

"You could leave him." There were few really good reasons Custis Long could think of for a woman to leave her husband. Wife beating might be among them. Child beating damn sure was. "You could leave the son of a bitch," he said.

Jane shook her head. "I couldn't, Custis. You know me better than that."

"The words and the promises don't seem to have meant all that much to Brent."

"They do to me," Jane said.

They sat in silence for some time, immersed in private thoughts. Longarm had no idea what hers might have been, but his were out of place in a man who was supposed to uphold the law. At the moment, he was more interested in breaking laws than maintaining them.

"I'm sorry I said anything, Custis," Jane said finally.

"I understand," he told her. "It's a terrible thing to have to hold inside yourself. And you couldn't hardly talk about it with just anybody. You know that I care a great deal for you and that little boy. I just wish I knew of a way to help that wouldn't leave you and Donny vulnerable to the son of a bitch afterward." He shook his head. "Sure had me fooled, he did. I thought he was about as fine a fella as you could hope to meet. Hell, I was really happy for the two of you."

Jane sighed. "Brent is a good man, in his own way. He is very good with people, very good for the community. He treats his men well, makes sure the mine is as safe as it can possibly be. He genuinely does care about people. Even about Donny and me, I think. It's just that he . . . gets frustrated. And at home is where he takes out those frustrations. With his fists or his belt." She began to cry again.

"I just wish . . ." His voice died away. He simply did not know how to help. A beating, which was what he would sorely like to give Brent MacRae, would only leave Jane and Donny in worse shape once Longarm was gone. A killing . . . the temptation was there, but only in the abstract. That was not Longarm's way. He had been a peace officer too long to allow it, he guessed. He shook his head. He just did not know what he could do.

"I feel better just from being able to talk to you about it, Custis." She gave him a weak smile. "You were Charlie's closest friend, and mine too, after we were married. I am grateful to you, Custis. I really am."

"Damn it, Jane, if there is ever anything you need— I mean *any*thing—you come to me and I'll help you. I'll give you train money East right this minute if you'll take Donny and go. You still have kin in Missouri?"

"Yes, but that isn't the answer. I remember the words very well, you know. I've thought about them often enough. 'For better or worse.' Well, this happens to be

47

'worse.' Maybe 'better' will come later." She smiled again, bravely, if not very convincingly.

"You remember what I said, Jane. Anything I can do for you, I will. Anything, any time. All you have to do is let me know."

"I'll remember, Custis." She smiled. "Thank you. And I know you have to get on. You can't dawdle around here all day when you have work to do. And I do thank you for being patient with me. You're a good friend, Custis. Thank you for that most of all."

Longarm did not want to leave. He felt an urge to stay and protect Jane and her son. But she was Brent MacRae's lawful wife and no man, deputy United States marshal or not, had any right to interfere with what he did in the privacy of his own home. Longarm collected his hat and let himself out the front door with a heavy heart.

Chapter 6

Fairplay was situated on the banks of the South Platte near its high-country headwaters. Buena Vista, separated from South Park by a mountain range, sat beside the Arkansas near *its* high-country headwaters, in a long, grassy valley between the Mosquito and the Collegiate ranges.

Longarm left the train there, for all practical purposes as track's end until the line completed its construction work north to Leadville and on west through the series of mountain ranges that rolled toward the setting sun like so many gigantic waves frozen in craggy granite. The setting was spectacular.

The stationmaster directed Longarm to the sheriff's office. The sheriff was an open-faced, pleasant-looking man, the kind who would win friends and votes easily on the basis of his personality. Quite often, Longarm knew, that kind was a wow at gaining office and a bust once installed.

"Pleased to meet you, Longarm," the sheriff said when

Longarm introduced himself. He shoved his hand forward. "I'm Ed Chapman. Kinda in charge around here at the local level. You work for Billy Vail?"

"Yes, sir."

Chapman smiled. "Next time you see that old scoundrel, you tell him I said hello. I don't get down-country very often, but the next time I do, I think I'll stop in there and collect some of the drinks he owes me." Chapman gave Longarm a conspiratorial wink. "If you ever need a free drink, son, remember that Billy's a sucker for a horseback shooting contest. Can't turn one down, but can't win one neither."

"You know Billy?"

"I should hope so. We rode together down in Texas a long while back, before he started sucking at Uncle's hind tit an' I started feeding at the county's trough."

Longarm grinned. It seemed his estimation of Sheriff Ed Chapman had been colored by an unfair comparison with that dimwit back in Fairplay. There were times, and this was one of them, when Longarm was grateful for the drawing of county lines.

"Now what can I do to help you, Longarm?" the sheriff asked.

Longarm explained.

"Hmmm." Chapman rubbed his chin, freshly shaved and still smelling of bay rum. "There's little enough I can tell you. The boy's dead, all right. Got confirmation of the identity from a brother who's living here. I wired that out to Billy and to the railroad. The road wired back this morning that they'd pay the reward. It should've come in on the same train you rode up."

"Have you seen the wanted list, Sheriff?"

"Ed, please. No, I haven't. I understand it's being held kind of close, actually. Don't know why, but the railroad seem to've put a lot of faith in these hired killers of theirs." He sighed. "And I'd be grateful if you'd kind of keep it to yourself that I said that. The railroad is stinkin' cheese around here, which I got to live with."

"These—uh—pet killers of theirs—are they railroad detectives?"

"Not really. They aren't bonded by the line or officially hired as far as I've been told, but I understand they have a hell of a reputation for getting a job done."

"Who are they?"

"I . . . hell, here they are. I'll introduce you."

Chapman started to speak as the two men entered his office, but the nearer of them began talking before the sheriff could do more than open his mouth.

"Where's my money, Edwin?" he asked belligerently. He stalked into the room and planted himself in front of Chapman's desk with an arrogant stance. The other man was silent.

Longarm folded his arms and took his time about looking them over. The one who had spoken was a lean man with a heavily seamed face and the bulbous, red-veined nose that comes from too much dissipation. His clothing was of decent cut but long in need of cleaning. Under his coat Longarm could see a short-barreled revolver carried in a cross-draw holster to the left of his belt buckle, a rig much like Longarm's, and on his right hip there was the bulge of a larger revolver.

The second man was shorter and stockier and even grimier in appearance. He too wore a brace of pistols, one with a short barrel for speed and a second with a longer barrel for accuracy.

One damned deadly duo, Longarm thought.

"Deputy, this gentleman—" Chapman was not a man for pretenses; he made no effort to conceal his contempt—"is Tyrone Broe. His partner is Nick Moore. Gentlemen, this is Deputy U. S. Marshal Long, working out of the Denver office of the Justice Department."

Broe gave Longarm a contemptuous look and did not

stick his hand out for a shake. Longarm got the impression the man would want to spit at him but not to shake his hand.

That was reasonable. Longarm had the same inclination himself.

Broe looked back at the sheriff. "Where's my money, Edwin?"

"You asked that once already," Chapman said mildly.

"I ain't heard an answer yet."

"In due time."

"Now!" Broe demanded.

"When it gets here."

"I already heard the money was bein' sent up. The damn train's in. So where's my money?"

"I sent a courier to pick it up. When he gets here, I will cheerfully turn the reward over to you." Chapman smiled. "It will be a pleasure. Because then you will leave immediately afterward."

"You damn well *better* turn it over," Broe muttered. He turned away with obvious disgust. "I hate waitin' around."

"One of life's little crosses," Longarm said.

"I didn't ask you nothin'."

"That's right, you didn't. But there was something I wanted to ask you," Longarm said. He had been doing some thinking since Chapman mentioned the bounty hunter's name. He knew he had heard it before. Now he thought he could remember what it was he had heard. "Didn't you used to work out of the San Francisco division, Broe? Carrying a badge just like mine?"

Broe glared at him but did not answer.

"I thought the name sounded familiar." Longarm accepted the silence as an admission.

"A federal marshal? *Him?*" Chapman asked.

"He never mentioned it to you? I reckon I'm not too surprised at that," Longarm said. "Mr. Broe here was— well, the polite way they put it was that his employment was no longer deemed necessary. To put it bluntly, he was fired. Would have gone to jail to boot, if he hadn't had some influential friends in the right places. Although how he managed to find any friends is beyond me."

Longarm was smiling tightly at the furious Broe. "Deputy Broe is a man with a bad temper and a fast trigger. It was bad enough that he had a habit of bringing his prisoners in dead, but it was too much when he took it on himself to shoot up a whorehouse in Sacramento. Killed two of the girls, the way I heard it. Of course, they were only whores. Apparently, that made a difference too. What was it they said to offend you, Tyrone?"

Longarm had turned to face Broe while he was talking. Now he stood poised, ready for the man to reach for the yellowed ivory grips of the revolver at his waist. The story he had just told Chapman was true, if not entirely provable. Longarm was hoping Broe would regard it as insulting as well.

He did. One look into those murderous, pale gray eyes was enough to prove that. Tyrone Broe, former deputy federal marshal, would gladly have cut Custis Long's liver out and fed it to the alley dogs in Buena Vista. Tension corded his neck and brought a bright flush of heat to his face. But he stood immobile and his hand never moved.

"No rebuttal, Tyrone?"

Broe remained silent.

"You surprise me," Longarm said.

"I don't like you, you prick," Broe snarled.

Longarm smiled. "You surprise me again. I hadn't expected you to pay me a compliment, but by damn I reckon you just did. The fact is, I don't like you a whole hell of a lot either. *Or* your trained monkey, there." Longarm hooked a thumb toward the still silent Nick Moore.

Moore obviously did not have the control that Broe did. He grunted something too low for Longarm to hear, and his right hand began to move.

Before Moore could reach for his gun, though, Broe was standing in the way, his left hand clamped on Moore's wrist.

No words passed between them. Apparently none had to. Moore silently accepted Broe's command. He held his hands out to the side, far away from his revolvers, and turned to stomp angrily out of the sheriff's office, leaving Broe behind.

"You don't show much respect for decent citizens," Broe accused. "I ought to report you to your superiors."

"Go right ahead," Longarm invited. "You know the chain of command as well as I do. Do anything you like, but stay the hell out of my way. I have work to do here, and I don't want the likes of you getting in my way. Understand me, Broe? If you step the least bit out of line, I'll have you in irons on a charge of obstruction of justice. I'd be real happy to do that. Any little excuse and I put the cuffs on your wrists, mister."

Broe sneered at him and spat on Ed Chapman's floor. "I don't figure to do anything outside the law, Deputy. Not a thing. But don't go thinkin' you can give me any orders neither. I know my rights an' I'll use every one of them. An' there's not a thing you can do about that."

Longarm wanted to have it out with Tyrone Broe, but until or unless Broe stepped out of line there was not a damn thing he could do. And both of them knew it.

The sheriff's courier arrived with a sealed money sack bearing the railroad's initials. Chapman opened it and dumped the pouch of gold coins onto his desk. He would have gone through the proper procedure of counting it and having the count witnessed, but Broe did not give him time. The bounty hunter grabbed the release form that had been delivered with the money, scrawled his signature on it, and took the money before Chapman had a chance to open the pouch.

"Stay out of my way," he shot over his shoulder as

he stormed out of the office.

"An' you out of mine," Longarm said softly behind him.

"Nice fella," the sheriff said.

"Ed, you don't know what a pleasure it is to be dealing with someone who actually wants to help for a change," Longarm said.

"Don't get to feeling too good about it until we do you some good, son," the sheriff said. "Still, my boys are pretty fair hands, and they keep their eyes and ears open. I'll get this list out to them right away, and if any of them knows anything I should have their reports by morning."

"You're a good man, Sheriff Chapman."

"True," Chapman agreed with a grin.

His best bet, Longarm had decided, and had confided without hesitation to Ed Chapman, would be to spot some of the remaining gang members and see if keeping tabs on one of them would bring him any closer to the unknown leader with the hood and the too-clever plans for robbery.

It had been Chapman who suggested that this deputies could lend assistance. It was impossible to keep track of every man who passed through the high-country mining camps, but a good peace officer has an instinct for those who bear watching. Chapman assured Longarm that his county deputies were boys who had those instincts, or they would not remain long on the payroll.

"I don't have enough of a budget to keep a bunch of yahoos for political purposes, so I made it plain from the start," the sheriff said. "If they ain't willing to do the work—an' that means all of it, good and bad alike—then they're welcome to draw their pay from the bridge-buildin' crews or whatever, but they shouldn't look for any here."

Longarm believed him.

"I'll get these names right out," Chapman said. "Check back with me in the morning." He smiled. "I'd have you over to the house for dinner this evening, but the commissioners are getting together tonight, an' I have to be there to make sure my department's backside is covered."

"Well, Billy doesn't like me let loose on the streets much without a keeper, Ed, but I reckon I can tough it out for one night," Longarm said with a grin.

"You do that." The county sheriff was immersed in a pile of paperwork before Longarm reached the front door.

There was, Longarm reflected, a world of difference between the good and the bad when it came to public officials. Buena Vista seemed to have drawn a good one.

He had left his gear with the DSP&P stationmaster, so he headed over that way to collect his Winchester and saddle and bag. Then he had to find a hotel.

The choices were not particularly limited, but they seemed far from luxurious. With the railroad construction going on and the constant flow of hopeful men into the mining camps, beds were at a premium in the newly expanding town. Longarm inspected several offerings and found them wanting except for lice. Most of them seemed to have an ample supply of livestock in their bedding.

Finally he found a respectable-looking frame house on a side street with a sign out front claiming they had rooms to rent. He presented himself at the front door and knocked with hat in hand.

"Ma'am," he said to the woman who answered his knock, "I sure hope you are willing to accommodate short-term guests."

The woman took her time looking him over. Longarm politely returned the courtesy.

She was slightly plump and full-figured. She reminded Longarm of the pictures frequently hung above saloon mirrors. She was dressed a bit better than any of those, though. Her hair was pinned up in a tight bun, and she wore a plain, matronly dress that tried but failed to conceal the ripe swell of bosom and hip above and below a more than ample waist. Longarm guessed her to be somewhere in the neighborhood of her thirties, if toward the shantytown end of that neighborhood.

He gave her his most winning and innocent smile. She was assessing him damned thoroughly, peering at him down the length of her nose.

"Please, ma'am? A man doesn't get much rest when he has to fight bedbugs the whole night through, and I can tell that a lady like you wouldn't allow anything unclean under her roof."

She fought it for a moment, but then she softened. Her head lost that backward tilt of impending refusal, and she gave him a hint of a smile. "I expect I could, just this once. Fifty cents a night, though. In advance."

Longarm smiled. "I don't know how long I'll have to be in town. Would it be all right if I just gave you a half-eagle deposit?"

Her smile was quite full this time. That was ten days' lodging. "That would be fine, Mr. . . . ?"

"Long, ma'am. Custis Long, of Denver."

"I am Mrs. Albertson, Mr. Long. If you will follow me, I'll show you to your room."

"Yes, ma'am." Longarm was pleased. The battle of the bedbugs would not have to be waged.

Better yet, the room came with a decently prepared and abundantly offered supper included. Longarm enjoyed it thoroughly, then leaned his chair back from the table and lighted a cheroot.

He thought about going out to investigate the nighttime offerings of Buena Vista, but decided against it. He had a nearly untapped bottle of Maryland rye in his bag, and after a night spent thrashing on Chen Li's bunk what he needed now was sleep. A few jolts from the jug, maybe one more cheroot, and he would be set for the duration.

There were seven other men at Mrs. Albertson's long table, and Longarm let their talk flow around him without paying any particular attention to it while he enjoyed his smoke. After a few minutes he became aware that someone was speaking to him.

"Sorry. What was that again?" he asked.

"I asked your opinion of the governor of this state, sir." The man asking the question was leaning forward in his chair and blinking owlishly. A whiff of his breath told Longarm that the fellow had had a moist afternoon.

"Sorry. I don't have an opinion."

"Nonsense," the man protested. "Everyone has an opinion. I merely ask for yours, sir."

Longarm shook his head.

The tipsy diner insisted.

"Sorry, sir. I'm a federal employee. It isn't my place to give opinions about state officers."

"Federal employee? What kind of federal employee? That's what I'm asking you, sir." The man blinked rapidly and aimed a finger toward Longarm's mustache.

"It isn't important," Longarm said, thinking that he had smoked about enough of his cheroot for the time being.

"Course it is, man. You work for me. I'm asking you now. Want to know what kind of federal employee can't offer an opinion. Y'know?" The fellow was swaying in his chair. Longarm wondered if he was about to topple into the mashed potatoes.

"C'mon," the fellow demanded.

"Deputy United States marshal," Longarm told him.

"Humph," the man snorted. "Your 'pinion wouldn't count for anything nohow, then." He turned and began questioning his seatmate to the other side.

Mrs. Albertson, seeming flustered about something,

got up hurriedly from the table and headed for the kitchen. Whatever it was she had forgotten, Longarm thought, he did not want to stay and have any. He excused himself before the tipsy gentleman could find some new excuse to share his bad breath with Longarm.

The thought of a closed door and an open bottle was becoming more and more attractive. Those and a long, deep night's sleep.

Chapter 7

It was something like drowning and having a wet dream at the same time. At his age? Couldn't be.

Longarm came awake with a yelp of surprise.

"Shhhhh!"

He was being smothered by—drowning in?—a warm, slightly damp mass that smelled like—he sniffed—scented powder.

He took a deep breath, feeling totally disoriented. He must be still asleep and having a nightmare, he told himself.

He opened his mouth to say something—he was not sure what: an exclamation, a protest, simply a good, hearty cussword suitable for multiple purposes—and the warm, moist mass flowed into his mouth.

He thought about biting but decided against that. It felt—well—alive.

His tongue touched a protrusion. Instinctively he rolled the turgid lump around on the end of his tongue.

It was a nipple.

Whose?

He had been alone when he went to sleep. He was *sure* of that. Almost sure. No, damn it, positive.

Besides, Li's entire *chest* wouldn't cover him the way this pair of pillow-sized tits was doing.

And Li was back in Fairplay. He wasn't in Fairplay now, was he? No. He was in Buena Vista.

He reached up to make sure with his hands. They were tits, all right. He squeezed one.

"That feels nice, honey."

That voice. Should he remember it? Whether he should or not, he didn't.

Hell, he told himself, a man ought to remember who he's sleeping with.

He thought about it some more and decided quite firmly that he *had* gone to sleep alone. In the boarding house in Buena Vista he'd had supper, had a couple of knocks from the bottle of Maryland rye. He was very tired.

Now he was awake. He felt groggy and light-headed, the way one feels when he is dragged out of the deepest sleep of exhaustion, long before any real rest has come.

"Such a fine-looking gentleman," the voice said.

The nipple was withdrawn, the soft pillows of flesh lifted, and Longarm could breathe again.

He felt a light touch at his crotch, a gentle exploration. In spite of himself, in spite of the confusion that was banging hollowly inside his logy skull, Longarm's manhood rose to the occasion without his direction.

"Lovely," the voice said. "Simply lovely. So nice and long."

That struck a chord: Li's teasing about his Chinese-modified name. But this was not Li and this was not Fairplay, and he did not know what anything or anyone was at the moment. He swallowed, tasting stale tobacco and stale rye whiskey, wishing whoever this woman was

62

she would light a lamp so he could reestablish contact with reality.

Well, maybe not *right* away...

The gentle fingertip touch at his crotch was replaced with a much more encompassing, wetter, hotter application of flesh to flesh.

What was she doing now? he wondered. Whatever it was, it felt good.

Whoever it was.

A soft, plopping slurp of sound told him which end was up. In this case, which end was down.

A French lesson, that was what this was.

Longarm shook his head, hoping to clear away the fog he was drifting in. It didn't seem to help.

The slurping sounds continued with slow regularity. So did the accompanying—and excellent—sensations.

"Mmmm."

Longarm did not answer. He would not have known what to say.

On the other hand, he was beginning to come fully awake now. He shook his head again, and kept his own mouth shut. Hers certainly was not, although it was wrapped rather tightly and was quite full at the moment. He wondered what he ought to do.

Whoever this woman was, and however she had gotten into his room, she was not attacking him or threatening him. Not hardly. He felt a spasm of increased arousal deep in his balls. It would seem damned indelicate to interrupt her now with questions.

He lay back, checked to assure himself that his double-action Colt was still hanging holstered by his head on the bedpost, and waited to see what would happen next.

What was happening next was very nice, he decided.

The slurping halted, and he felt the warmth being withdrawn. The spittle left exposed on his shaft felt chill. But only for a moment.

He could feel the mattress tilt as weight shifted down there—rather a lot of weight, he judged—and a pair of hefty thighs straddled him as he lay on his back.

"Let's try it this way for a while, honey."

He really should be able to recognize that voice, he thought. He felt that he had heard it before. But where?

The weight pressed down over him, and once again he was engulfed by flesh. He could feel bristly, wire-tight curls of hair around the root of his shaft. Warm and wet. A different warmth and a different moisture from what he had been feeling a moment ago.

Not particularly tight, though. Certainly not in Li's class. He wondered briefly if the Chinese girl had spoiled him for normal pleasures with normal women.

Well, perhaps not. This wasn't Li—but this wasn't bad, either.

He felt hands bracing the woman, the hands at Longarm's sides, and she began to rock back and forth, pulling him out of the warm, cavernous, unseen opening, and jamming him back in again.

No, not bad, he thought.

His body stiffened in an involuntary reflex, and the woman's rocking motion became more pronounced. She speeded her efforts, then slowed them, and finally stopped altogether.

"Not yet," she whispered. "Not quite yet, honey." She chuckled. Or maybe it was a giggle. He was not sure. "You sure are ready, though, aren't you?"

She dismounted and slid off the side of the bed.

Was that it? he wondered. Possibly this might be the time to ask her who the hell she was.

No. She was busy again. Kneeling beside the bed this time. Going back to her pursuit of oral French. If she was not Li's equal in the one category, she was damned good in the other. Longarm felt himself building again. She stopped.

"Not so soon, honey. We don't want to be in a hurry here."

The damned woman was keeping him hanging on the brink, but wouldn't let him over the edge. Time and time again she brought him up, a flick of the tongue here, a deep intake there, and every time he built there was the sudden release, the chill of night air on wet, recently abandoned flesh.

Longarm reached down and pressed against the back of her head. He wanted her to stay there for a change, and he also thought the exploration might give him a clue as to who she was.

No help at all. The hair was an untidy nest of hair. The face was only a face. He could not begin to identify it by touch. And damned if she didn't pull away again, in spite of his urging.

He felt her tongue lapping busily at the sensitive area between his balls and his ass. Nice enough, but not leading toward the conclusion he was by now aching to achieve.

"Lovely," she said.

"Thank you," he told her.

She chuckled.

Distantly, somewhere downstairs in the boarding house, he heard a door slam. The woman rejoined him on the bed, once again straddled him, and took him into her.

Downstairs someone was singing. A loud, off-key, quite drunken voice. It was distracting.

The woman began to pump back and forth with vigor now. On the thin mattress and rickety springs of the boardinghouse bed it was something like being at sea in a rowboat during a storm. The bed was making as much noise as the drunk. That was distracting, too.

Still, she had kept him at a high peak too long for him to ignore these vigorous sensations now. He built again quickly, shuddered, and made a convulsive upward lunge with his hips to drive himself fully into her as the heat spilled out of him and into her.

He bucked upward violently.

His lunge caught the woman off balance. She fell off him, off the side of the bed, and landed with a solid thump on the hardwood flooring.

"Ow!"

"Are you all right, ma'am?" It sounded ridiculous to him, even at the time, but what the hell was he *supposed* to call her?

"I think so." She was groaning.

Longarm swung his legs off the side of the bed, found the box of matches where he had left them on the bedside table, and touched one to the lamp.

"Mrs. Albertson!"

She smiled. "Mr. Long."

"Good grief." He was sorry he had lighted the lamp. Without her clothing, Mrs. Albertson did not at all resemble a saloon nude painting. Mrs. Albertson was damn well fat.

Longarm stood and jumped for his trousers draped over the back of a chair, ignoring the thin stream of white, sticky fluid that was oozing down the inside of his thigh. He pulled his pants on. He felt embarrassed, even though he could not think why *he* should be the one feeling any embarrassment. Downstairs the drunk was still singing.

"Why did you put your trousers on, Mr. Long? Wouldn't you enjoy some more loving? A little..."

"Mrs. Albertson, *please*."

"Yes, Marshal, please. Come back to this comfy bed." She patted it for emphasis. "You don't need those trousers now, do you? Of course not." She reached toward him. "Let me show you what I can do for a virile man like yourself. Take those trousers off now. Please."

Longarm twisted away from her. She followed, trying to reach his fly and undo the buttons he was fumbling to fasten.

"Take them off now, please."

"Mrs. Albertson, you're a married lady," he protested. He refrained from adding that she was a damned undesirable one too, now that he could see her. He shook his head.

"Please, Marshal, don't go out anywhere. Come back to bed, honey."

Longarm loped across the room, putting the width of the bed between them.

For the first time he had a moment to wonder why a married and presumably respectable—and homely; he hardly needed to remind himself of that—woman would be so intent on romping the night away with a total stranger. This was hardly normal behavior in any boardinghouse he had ever heard of. This one had seemed as ordinary and as respectable as any other until now.

She had come in uninvited, with a passkey no doubt, and made love to him in the dark. Oddly, too, now that he thought about it. All that building and releasing and finally all that banging and clattering toward the end. He certainly would have thought, if she was the kind who gave it away to strangers—*forced it on them* would be more accurate—she would not want anyone to hear.

Hear. Hearing works two ways. And he remembered that just before all that loud thrashing, he had heard that drunk come in downstairs. The drunk was awake, obviously, and must have heard them.

Strange, Longarm thought. But maybe he was not supposed to have heard the drunk.

Longarm felt weary. He thought he finally knew what all this was about.

"Mrs. Albertson."

"Yes, Marshal?"

"What is your husband wanted for, ma'am?"

The woman's face crumbled. Big tears began to roll down her round cheeks.

"What is it, ma'am?"

She swallowed. "Forgery. Back in Iowa, it was." She looked stricken at the enormity of it. "He's a good man, Marshal, he's..."

Longarm held his hand up to stop her. He felt sad for her. She was a pitiable figure, standing there fat and naked and crying. He wished she had not done this.

"That's not a federal crime, ma'am. I don't want to take your husband away from you, and..." He paused. Christ, he would just make matters worse for the poor thing if he kept on the way he had intended, like telling her the truth.

"Ma'am," he said, "he's wanted in Iowa, but I don't actually have any *federal* papers on him. And I reckon after what you did— well, I could just forget that he's here. You understand. It wouldn't do for my boss to hear what's been going on here. So I'll make a deal with you. If you don't say anything, I won't either."

The look on Mrs. Albertson's face told him that he was right to let her go on thinking that he could have arrested her husband. At least now she could retain some small measure of pride for having saved her husband from jail.

"Take a bath, ma'am," he said gently. "You'll feel better. And go back to your husband. I won't take him in. Tomorrow I'll move to another place. All right?"

She nodded. The poor woman looked grateful to him. Then she began to look sly. She drew herself to her full height and now was able to look down her nose at the bribed federal deputy. She dressed with as much dignity as a naked fat lady could manage and sniffed her way out of the room, obviously convinced that her sacrifice had worked.

Longarm shook his head. He locked the door behind

her and sat on the edge of the bed. He wanted to laugh, but he felt sad at the same time. *People,* he thought wearily.

He leaned forward to blow out the lamp and lay back on the warm, rumpled sheets of the hired bed.

People.

He went back to sleep quickly.

Chapter 8

Sheriff Ed Chapman apparently was not a man who be-grudged the time he gave to the taxpayers who had voted for him. He was already in his office when Longarm arrived there the next morning, and Longarm was an early riser himself. The sheriff greeted the federal deputy with a poker face.

"Well?" Longarm asked. He settled himself in a chair before the sheriff's desk and pulled a cheroot from his pocket.

"Your friendly neighborhood train robbers were busy again yesterday," Chapman said. "They hit the evening up-bound. Stopped it between Como and Red Hill Pass. According to the wire that was waiting on my desk this morning, they took two payroll chests and walked away clean. The same old crowd, they figure. The robbers never even looked at the mail car. But there is some good news...."

Longarm uttered some carefully selected epithets. Bad luck and worse timing. If he had taken the late train to Buena Vista instead of the midday, he would have been on hand when the robbery took place. He might have been able to stop it. Instead he was lollygagging around in comfort while two mine payrolls were being carted off by a group of happy robbers.

Sons of bitches, he thought sourly. He did not entirely exclude himself from that expression of disgust.

"I did say there was good news too," Chapman reminded him.

"The way today's starting out," Longarm said, "you'll likely tell me next that you were lying just to make me feel better."

Chapman smiled. "It could be worse, you know."

"Don't suggest that, or it probably *will* be."

The sheriff shrugged, took a piece of paper from his desk, and tossed it idly into a drawer. "If you don't want to hear it . . ."

"I want to. I want to hear it."

He retrieved the paper. "What I have here is your list of names. Five of them, one of whom is now deceased and the appropriate reward duly paid." He smiled grimly. "I kind of hope the railroad shortchanged the son of a bitch. Not that it's any of my concern, of course."

"Are you going to take all day with this?"

"I'm thinking about it."

Longarm rolled his eyes heavenward. He also kept his mouth shut, deciding that was the only way to deal with Ed Chapman early in the morning.

"Anyway," the sheriff said, "my fine fellows out in the field have come up with leads on three of these other gentlemen."

"Really?" Longarm took his cheroot out of his mouth and sat up straighter. It was about time they got a break in this case.

"Would I lie to a federal officer, I ask you?"

"Hell yes, you would, but that's beside the point. Which names?"

"Bert Chambliss. He's the first one on your list. According to my boys he has a lady-love up in Leadville. Somewhat soiled, buy nonetheless lovable. He hasn't been seen in several days, but the lady friend is still there, and I understand he never stays away from her very long."

Longarm was grinning. "That's perfect. Young Gay says this Bert is out best lead to the man in the hood. Who else?"

"Peter Casey. He shares a cabin with a prospector up in the Collegiates. They might be related somehow; my boy isn't sure. He doesn't know if Casey is there now or not, as he hasn't been over that way in a couple weeks."

Longarm nodded. So far, so good. Pete Casey was the one who had recruited Tris Gay into the gang. He too should make a good lead.

"The last one is Charles Winter, also known as Iceman. My boys say he divides his time between Leadville and Mosquito Gulch. That's out of my jurisdiction, of course, but my boys have big ears. Again, we don't know for sure if he's been around lately. I am also told that his nickname has nothing to do with a play on his last name. Apparently the Iceman is one cold-blooded son of a bitch."

"You and your people do good work, Sheriff," Longarm said sincerely.

"I'll take that as a compliment, Deputy."

"It was damn well intended as one."

"Could I make a suggestion?" Chapman asked. "Or an offer?"

"Of course." Longarm had no false pride when it came to accepting advice from fellow professionals, and Ed Chapman was clearly a professional.

"You can't cover all of them by yourself. I'd be glad to assign one or two of my people to help you. It is, after all, in the interests of the railroad and the mines up here."

73

"I appreciate that, Ed." Longarm thought for a moment. "I want to take this Bert Chambliss myself. He seems to be our best bet for getting at the head of this particular snake. And Winter is probably holed up over in Park County. But if you could have someone keep a watch over Pete Casey, it could be a big help."

"I'll issue the order this morning. My man who knows him is Rick Jamison. I'll tell him to report to you on this and to take orders from you if need be. He's a good man."

Longarm was overwhelmed. Cooperation between local and federal officers was one thing, but this was exceptional. He was beginning to think that things were about to break for him.

Chapter 9

Leadville was a town of extremes. Busier, noisier, and more boisterous than Buena Vista and Fairplay combined, yet it was more barren than Hell itself. Every scrap of available timber for miles around had been cut for shaft shores or for the countless fires that kept a gray pall over the craggy countryside, fires for cooking and at night for heat even during the supposedly temperate summer months, fires day and night in the smelters that lined the muddy smear that was the mighty Arkansas here. More men, more money, and more sin than even a veteran lawman would have guessed in such a remote location.

And much, much less breathable air.

In addition to the sting of the smoke deep in his lungs, Longarm found himself gasping for breath from the briefest and least strenuous of exertions. Leadville was at an altitude Longarm considered barely fit for human habitation.

Rather than carry his gear any distance in that thin

atmosphere, he checked into the closest hotel to the stage stop and gladly paid two dollars of the government's money for a room that should have cost a quarter that amount. At least, he discovered, the attached saloon carried a decent brand of Maryland rye. At the time it seemed like ample compensation for any other shortcomings the busy place might have.

He locked himself into the privacy of his room tilted the single rickety chair against the wall with his feet propped on the lumpy bed, and took a long pull of the good rye.

According to what Ed Chapman had told him, Bert Chambliss hung out frequently at a State Street parlor house called the Beezle Bub. It sounded enchanting, Longarm thought sourly. It also sounded like a place where a deputy United States marshal would be anything but welcome.

A man could waste hours in a saloon or a gambling hall without causing comment, but there are damn few reasons for a man to spend time in a whorehouse. Custis Long could hardly be considered a prude, but he was not particularly pleased with the idea—and was not the kind of man who found it necessary, in any event—of buying women on the hoof.

The surveillance would have been easier, he thought, if Leadville was the kind of place to mix the businesses available in its State Street attractions. Or if that damned Chambliss had chosen some other place to find himself a girl friend.

Still, the Beezle Bub was the place he had to keep an eye on if he wanted Chambliss to lead him to the man in the powder-bag hood.

Longarm admired the color of the liquor in his bottle, shook his head, and rammed the cork back into the mouth of the jug. He settled for a cheroot. A clear head was going to be a necessity if he expected to accomplish anything here.

The hotel clerk, a one-armed man with a heavy accent and pain in his dark eyes, gave Longarm directions to "the Bub" without hesitation.

The place turned out to be hardly distinguishable from any of the others lined up along the wide, open strip that served Leadville's raucous needs day and night. It was a tall, narrow, false-fronted structure with tarpaper walls where canvas must once have been.

Longarm was greeted in the foyer by a pale, heavy-set woman who he assumed was the madam. She was, predictably enough, overjoyed to see him.

"Welcome to our little place of comfort, Mr. . . . ?"

"Long," he answered without thinking. If he had had a moment to anticipate the question he might have given a false name. Now it was too late.

"Is that a name or a description?" the old bawd asked with a leer and a wink.

He forced a smile. "A name, I'm afraid." He would much prefer to be with Chen Li now, where the name-play would have been going on with genuine affection and warmth.

"My girls will be sorry to hear that," the madam said with another wink. "But you're a handsome devil anyway. I don't think they'll be disappointed."

"Let's hope not," Longarm said, trying to force an eagerness he did not feel into his voice.

"I'll have to ask you to check your gun, Mr. Long. We have no need for weapons here, you understand. You are always among friends when you're under my roof."

"Yes, ma'am." Again taking care to hide his feelings, Longarm unbuckled his gunbelt and handed the woman the double-action .44 in its cross-draw holster. He did not consider it unethical to neglect to mention the der-ringer on his watch chain.

"Polite lad, aren't you?"

"Thank you."

"See?" For some reason, she went into a howling fit

of laughter. Longarm could see nothing funny in anything that had been said. He seriously questioned Bert Chambliss's taste. "Come along, Mr. Long," the madam went on.

"Yes, ma'am."

The parlor she led him into held a dozen men or more and only two whores, neither attractive in the slightest, both wearing more makeup than clothing. They were heavily painted but wore only high-heeled slippers and chemises over bodies so soft and pasty they reminded Longarm of unbaked biscuit dough. They were hardly the thing to set a man's blood afire, Longarm thought.

Still, he was going to have to pretend a love affair with *someone* in the damn place if he expected to find and to watch Mr. Bert Chambliss.

"Is this the entire—uh—selection?" he asked.

"Not at all, Mr. Long. We have eight lovely young ladies to provide for your comfort and relaxation here. The other ladies are all entertaining at the moment."

"You wouldn't mind if I got a look at all of them, then?"

"Please do." The old bag batted her eyelashes at him. "Your happiness is our only concern here, you understand. While you wait, feel free to refresh yourself. Drinks are a dime. Cigars and pipes of opium are priced as modestly, you will find. We—"

He cut her sales pitch short with a "Thank you" that he hoped sounded polite and slumped into an overstuffed armchair in a corner of the room.

The other men in the room, nearly all of them roughly dressed, were smoking and talking and sucking down liquor. One of the girls was surrounded by three miners, all trying to fondle her at the same time. The other girl was being led up a flight of stairs by another man.

Home away from home, Longarm thought.

He smoked a cheroot, smiled pleasantly whenever anyone looked in his direction, and kept his ears open to the use of names among the customers. He wished he knew which girl was Chambliss's lady-love, so that at least he would know which girl to watch closely. As it was, he had to play a waiting game. And that was hardly Longarm's idea of a good time.

The girls came and went, trooping up and down the stairs with monotonous regularity. Not one of them, Longarm thought, could even compare with poor, fat old Mrs. Albertson back in Buena Vista.

And judging from the number of times they went up those stairs, even a self-respecting boar hog would have to think twice. Sanitary they were not. Couldn't be. Longarm wondered if the line of duty was going to require him to contract a disease. He shuddered.

Maybe, he thought, a strong drink would help. He left the armchair and made his way through the room to the bar in a small adjoining room.

"Rye whiskey, please."

"Yes, sir." The person who answered was a surprise. Longarm had been expecting a burly bartender—surely there would have to be a strong-arm bouncer somewhere handy—but instead he was greeted by a fresh-faced, red-haired girl who had a scrubbed, just-off-the-farm look about her. Flame-bright tendrils of damp hair were escaping from her bun and falling over her ears. She wore no makeup, and needed none to accent the bright blue-green of her eyes. When she smiled he saw that her teeth were crooked, and one was missing entirely, but otherwise she was an attractive girl who could not yet have reached twenty.

She served him a generous splash of rye in a glass and picked up the dime Longarm laid on the bar. "Was there something else, sir?"

Longarm smiled at her. "Just marveling."

She laughed. "You mean, what is a nice girl like me doing in a place like this?"

"You've heard that question before, I take it?"

"Not more than twenty times a night," she said.

"And your answer?"

She shrugged. "Just your typical hard-luck story."

"I have time to listen to it, if you don't mind another telling."

"Oh, I don't mind. There isn't that much to tell. I came out here from back home. That's Iowa, by the way. Or it used to be. Anyway, I came out here to meet with my fiancé. He had come West to make our fortune. He sent for me when he found work, if not exactly a fortune. My father said if I ran off to meet him in this godless land I was no daughter of his. But I came anyway.

"By the time I arrived, my fiancé had died in a mining accident. I had to make my way alone. And Miss Emmalene was the only person kind enough to give me employment. So here I am. It isn't all that sad a story, actually, and certainly nor a rare one. It is my choice to work downstairs. There are those who think I should change my mind." She raised her eyebrows and waited expectantly, obviously waiting for him to join the ranks of men who were trying to change her mind.

Longarm took a sip of the rye. It was poor-quality stuff.

"No comment?" the girl asked.

"No point in it," he said. "I can't do a thing to change any of it, and my sympathy wouldn't buy you a ticket to the next town down the pike, much less back to Iowa. If you wanted a ticket, that is. I expect if you wanted one you'd have it by now. So I guess I don't have any comments to make, no."

She grinned at him. She looked rosy-cheeked and pretty when she smiled. "Thanks."

"For what?"

"For not offering to help me escape from a sinful life, I suppose." She giggled. "If only, that is, I would commit one or two minor sins in exchange."

"Is that the usual line?"

"Uh-huh."

"Sounds tiresome."

"It is, believe me."

He took another swallow of the substandard rye and made a face.

"I— uh — have another bottle back here that you might like better," the girl offered.

Longarm grinned at her. "I think I'd like a glass of coal oil better. Just as well, anyhow."

The girl looked around and gave him a conspiratorial wink. A wink looked much better on her face than it had on Miss Emmalene's. "Just don't tell."

"Cross my heart," he said in a mock whisper.

She emptied his glass into a bucket behind the bar and refilled it from another bottle bearing exactly the same label as the first.

Longarm tasted. "That's more like it," he said. "Thanks."

"You're quite welcome." She tilted her head and looked at him closely through lowered eyelids. "My name is Anna," she announced.

"Mine's—"

"Don't," she interrupted.

"What?"

"Don't tell me your name, please."

"All right." He was puzzled, and it showed, but he did not question her.

"You're all right, you know that?"

He smiled. "I'm proud you think so, Anna."

"Would you do something for me?"

He shrugged. "If I can."

"I have a sort of a fantasy. I don't want to tell you all about it. Not right now. Later, maybe, but not now." She paused and looked at him. He got the impression she was waiting for him to interrupt or to question her. He waited patiently for her to go on.

"Miss Emmalene owes me some time off," she said.

81

Again he waited until she was ready to continue.

"I could take the rest of the evening off. If you would walk home with me. And stay with me for a little while." She looked suddenly very shy. She began to blush. "In my bed."

"I'd be proud to, Anna," Longarm said seriously.

"Wait right here." She turned and darted out from behind the bar. She was smiling happily when she returned moments later.

Anna posed for his admiration at the foot of the bed, naked, moving slowly with her arms uplifted to unpin her hair and let it spill in a shimmering red flow down her flawless back. She turned to face him and stood with her chin high while Longarm looked at what he was being given.

Her body was full and soft but nicely curved. The skin of her breasts was as pale as skim milk and seemed almost translucent. He could see a network of blue veins through the tender covering of thin skin, and her nipples were small and of a pink so light it was difficult to distinguish them from the flesh of her breasts.

Her pubic hair was the same bright flame of red as the hair on her head, and her mound was prominent, her sex seeming to be tilted high and forward. *Convenient,* Longarm thought.

The girl's odd action in grabbing him out of the whorehouse and bringing him to her room in another house for free made him wonder if he was the lucky recipient of a lost wager or some other equally silly joke. Had there been a code word, perhaps, and the first girl to hear it had to give herself to whatever stranger spoke it? And there was that business about not wanting to know his name. *A bet? A dare?* he wondered. Not that he was complaining. Anna, whoever and whatever she was, whatever her odd reasons, was infinitely better than the sloppily over-used whores in the parlor.

Better yet, the girl might provide him with an excuse to hang around the Beezle Bub for days to come without having to dip his wick into any miner's leftovers.

"You're beautiful," he said. It was only partially a lie. She was genuinely attractive, if not actually beautiful.

Anna smiled. "Thank you."

Now that they were in her room, she seemed in no hurry about joining him on the bed. She crossed to her bureau and began to brush her hair. For a fresh-faced farm girl from Iowa, she seemed quite unconcerned about displaying her body. Longarm waited patiently for her to finish. When she came to him he slid obligingly aside to make room on the narrow bed.

"Would you mind kissing me?" she asked.

He nuzzled her face and waited the space of several breaths before he answered. "Not at all." It had been unnecessarily suspicious of him, he discovered, checking for the telltale scent of come on her breath, but he felt a little better for having done it.

The taste of her was young and sweet. She kissed him with enthusiasm if not with expertise. That surprised him, under the circumstances. But there was very little about this girl that was what he might have expected.

He ran his palm over her breasts and toyed with her nipples for a time before continuing his explorations lower. The skin of her lower belly was cool and incredibly soft. He played with the small button that was her clitoris and slid a probing finger inside her. She was so tight he could scarcely force his middle finger into her.

"You aren't a virgin, are you?"

Anna smiled and shook her head. "Alum," she explained.

Longarm accepted the explanation. It was a professional's trick to restore some grab to a tired box.

"Take me now, please," she said.

"You're in a hurry," he said.

83

"No. I just want to feel you inside me."

She let her legs fall apart and pulled him over her body, warming under his touching, and reached to guide him.

Longarm was still confused. Anna seemed a study in contrasts, both whorish and virginal at the same time.

A moment later he did not care.

The head of his tool slid into her, and the heat from her body was searing.

Damn it, though, he could only go an inch or two inside. There seemed to be a blockage of some sort. He stopped, unwilling to hurt her.

"Go ahead," she urged. "Too much alum, I guess."

Longarm leaned his weight against her. There was resistance for just a moment longer, then a distinct feeling of release. He plunged full length into her, and Anna cried out slightly. Her body was tense beneath him.

"Are you all right?"

"Yes. Yes." She was crying. "Thank you."

"What . . . ?"

"It's all right. Please. Go ahead now."

Puzzled but certainly willing—such tightness and such fierce heat, even his *balls* felt hot, were far beyond the ordinary—he began to pump gently in and out.

He rocked slowly back and forth, waiting for her to build, waiting for her to join him, but she seemed either unable or unwilling to do so.

And he could control his own increase in sensitivity only for so long. Consideration only goes so far, after all, and the hold she had on him was like being grasped in a hot, wet vise that was able to apply delightful pressure in every direction at once.

"I can't hold off much longer," he said.

"Good," Anna whispered happily. She wrapped her arms and legs around him and hung on while he began to stroke into her more and more quickly until he was ramming deep and fast, pounding her belly with his and trying to drive his cock so deep it would reach her throat the hard way there.

He spilled over the peak with a shuddering groan, and hot fluid pumped in violent spasms into her.

Anna was clinging to him like a leech, sobbing into his shoulder, but when he pulled back to look at her he could see she was crying with what seemed to be real happiness.

"Are you all right?"

"Oh, yes. Thank you. Thank you so much." She rubbed her face against the thick pad of muscle on his shoulder to wipe the tears away and lay smiling at him. She craned her neck high to kiss him.

Unusual, this girl; but quite sweet, he thought.

He began to withdraw from her, but she stopped him. "Not yet," she said.

"All right." He lay within her, taking his weight on his elbows, while Anna teased him with repeated contractions of the weak ringlet of muscles at the opening where he was limply captured.

"Does that feel nice?" she asked.

"Very."

"Good." She kissed him again. It did feel good, too. With practically no effort at all he would find himself ready to go another round.

She reached between their bellies and began to run her fingertips over the sensitive skin of his scrotum.

"In case you were wondering," he said, "that sure feels nice too."

Anna smiled. Her blue-green eyes widened and her smile changed in quality to a different kind of pleasure as she felt him rise and stiffen inside her. "Already?"

"Entirely because of you," he said gallantly.

She sighed and closed her eyes in contentment while once again Longarm began to stroke into her with long, slow, smooth thrusts.

He took longer the second time, and this time he

thought Anna had begun to build with him but again she did not, not quite, and for the second time the unusual tightness and heat of her body overcame his sense of control. Again he pounded her soft belly with his hard, male body, and she responded with joy when he bucked and shuddered to an explosive climax.

She was sobbing loudly this time when she kissed him deeply and thanked him over and over again.

"Believe me," he said, "the pleasure was mine."

She sniffled and wiped her eyes and nose with the back of her hand. "I'm so grateful to you."

It would have been impolite for him to show his amazement with this strange girl, but he damn sure felt it. She was a caution, that was for sure.

Completely limp and spent now, the contractions caused by her sobbing plopped him wetly out of her and he rolled off of her soft body. He ran his hand down her damp, slightly rounded belly and bent to pluck her nipple between his lips. A flash of scarlet seen out of the corner of his eye stopped him in mid-nibble.

Her hair was red, but not *that* red. He looked closer.

Anna's pubic hair was stained an even brighter red than it had been before. And there were stains along the insides of her thighs.

"You . . ."

"You wouldn't have done it if you'd known I was a virgin," she said calmly.

Longarm sat upright on the edge of the bed and glared at her. "Hell, no, I wouldn't have."

"Which is exactly why I lied to you," she said.

"But . . ."

"What's done is done, now. You can't take it back." She smiled. "And I still do thank you."

"But why? I mean, I know that story about the dead fiancé was a crock. But why this?" He shook his head. "I do not understand you, girl, whoever the hell you are."

Anna laughed. "I'm almost nineteen years old, work in a parlor house, and I'm still a virgin. Or was, until a few minutes ago. Thanks to you, I can now begin to earn a decent living for myself."

Longarm still did not understand and told her so.

"Oh, it isn't nearly as good a story as that one about my lost love from Iowa."

He waited for her to go on, and finally she shrugged.

"I've been with Miss Emmalene for as long as I can remember. She took me in when I was little. I've been around the business just about all my life, I guess, but somewhere I got it in my head to be scared of men's peckers. I ask you, isn't that the most awful thing you've ever heard? Supposed to be a proper whore and I get scared of a little ol' thing like a pecker." She smiled and stroked him. "Not that *you* are little, believe me."

"If you were a virgin, which I can damn well attest to now, how...?"

"Oh, I've been taught pretty well. All the girls've tried to help me. And some of our regular customers, too. I can give really grand hand jobs, and I can suck cock almost as good as Julie. She's our French expert. It's just fucking that I couldn't bring myself to do.

"So anyway, I made up my mind that when I met a nice, clean-looking gentleman who I thought would be gentle, why, he'd be the one. And I did it, too. Or you did. You just don't know how glad I am that you came in tonight." She was smiling merrily and seemed genuinely delighted.

"What was that business about not wanting to know my name?"

Anna blushed. "I told you it was a sort of fantasy. When I was just about old enough to start my monthlies I had a boy friend. His mama ran the parlor house next to ours over in Virginia City, Nevada, at the time. We messed around a lot, touching and feeling and kid stuff like that, but Miss Emmalene was real strict about me

87

not letting him have any. Not for real. She thought she could get a lot for me as a virgin, see, and she would have, if the old bastard who paid for me that first time hadn't had such a knobby pecker. I got scared of it and went to screaming and he got all upset and eventually Miss Emmalene had to give him his money back and give him a twosome free of charge just to keep his good will. I guess that's what got me off on the wrong track. Anyway, I'd told myself that I wanted the first time to be with him when he was all grown up. So when you were inside me a minute ago I was pretending it was him. You—uh—you aren't Billy Webber all grown up, are you?"

Longarm was not entirely sure if he should laugh or feel insulted. He decided it was better to laugh about it.

Fresh-faced, sweet and virginal. You bet.

"Anna," he said, "you are a downright unforgettable young lady."

"Thank you."

He remembered, though, that there was work to be done, and that he had a serious reason for being here. "Would you mind, now that you seem to be off to a good start, if I came to call on you again sometimes?"

"Of *course* not, sweetie. Please do." She smiled, and he noticed there were cute dimples in her cheeks when she did so. "It will be two dollars."

Chapter 10

Now that Anna had gone public, as it were, Longarm's ability to enjoy her company was greatly reduced. Several days of sharing her with every Leadville miner who had two dollars and a yen for something fresh was more than enough to alter Longarm's view of the girl.

Still, there was a job to be done, and in addition to her other qualities—not virtues, exactly, but qualities—she was a talkative little wench.

"A fella named Bert? Sure, he's sweet on Carrie. He's one of her regulars. He's in here whenever he has the money. Come to think of it, I haven't seen him in about a week now. He hardly ever stays away from her that long." She was cuddled up next to him, sweaty and happy, idly stroking his genitals while she chattered. The damned girl managed somehow to still convey that fresh-faced, girl-next-door quality. "What d'you want with ol' Bert? Or shouldn't I be asking?"

"Whyever shouldn't you ask?" Longarm asked in return.

"If you know Bert— Well, him and you are not

exactly the same sort, if you know what I mean."

"I don't know what you mean," Longarm said. "Don't know Bert either for that matter. A mutual friend suggested I look him up, that's all."

"I don't think you'd like ol' Bert. Can I tell you a secret?"

"Of course."

"Carrie doesn't like Bert either, not all that much. But he always tips her extra, and she squirrels that away without telling Miss Emmalene. I guess the more she loves up to him, the more he tips her, so she loves up to him pretty good."

"Not a nice fellow, though, huh?"

"Kind of creepy little bastard, really. Buck-toothed and hair like it came out of a rotted cornhusk. And he's kinda mean, too. I'm glad it's Carrie he's sweet on and not me."

Longarm grunted something appropriate and soothing. After all, he was supposed to be sweet on Anna, wasn't he? The thought was about enough to make a grown man sick.

At the same time, he was trying to remember which of the whores was Carrie. They all looked pretty much alike, in spite of differences of hair color and size. There was just something about them that made them all seem alike.

"Carrie," he said, "she's the girl with the light brown hair, isn't she?"

"No, silly." She reached up and gave him a moist kiss on the lips, which he did not appreciate—no telling where that mouth had been lately. She said, "But at least that shows you aren't paying attention to any of the other girls, sweetie."

Longarm croaked out the obligatory laugh.

"Carrie's the cute blonde with the little titties." She pressed her own ample breasts flat by way of demonstration.

Longarm remembered her then, more or less. He was going to have to pay closer attention when they returned to the parlor.

In the meantime, Anna did not seem to think their early evening entertainment was concluded. She bent to envelop him in the heat of her mouth. In spite of himself, Longarm felt an erection growing.

Anna looked up at him and grinned. "I surely do like the taste of you, sweetie."

Longarm smiled at her. What the hell, it was all in the line of duty. And it was the government's money, not his, that was being spent. He lay back and let Anna attend to him.

"Son of a bitch," Longarm muttered to himself when he read the telegraph message that had been waiting in his box at the hotel.

PETER CASEY DECEASED STOP BOUNTY HUNTER STOP ADVISE

It was signed by Sheriff Chapman's deputy, Rick Jamison. The point of origin was a town Longarm had never heard of called Blue Timber.

"Where's Blue Timber?" Longarm asked the desk clerk.

"If I remember correctly, it's a camp west of Buena Vista, up in the mountains there."

"Would the stage have connections there?"

The man shrugged. "I reckon."

There was a night coach going down the river, if Longarm remembered correctly. And, since Bert Chambliss had not yet showed up in Leadville, Longarm probably should go down there and find out more about Pete Casey and how the man came to be deceased. Damn it! Just when he thought things were going to straighten out on this case.

"I'll be checking out now," he said.

The desk clerk acted as though he would be able to

accept that fact without allowing it to devastate him.

Longarm sighed. The prospect of a night spent rattling around in a hard-sprung mud wagon was not his idea of a good time. Especially with a dead suspect at the other end of that trip. It was just so darn difficult to question a dead man.

He trudged up the stairs to get his gear.

"Jamison? I'm Custis Long." He shoved his hand out toward the slender, dark-haired man with the badge pinned to his vest.

"A pleasure, Marshal."

"Just a deputy, same as you," Longarm said.

Jamison grinned. "According to Ed Chapman, anybody who's riding for Billy Vail is plenty damned good or he doesn't last long."

"Not good enough this time, looks like. What happened here?"

Jamison made a face. "What it comes down to, Marshal, was legal murder—and I watched the whole thing happen. Couldn't do a thing about it." He turned and began leading Longarm down the path that served Blue Timber for a main street.

"Right over there's the only saloon in the camp." He pointed to a sagging tent with a hand-lettered sign hung from the ridgepole proclaiming drinks for a half bit. "I was there at the time, nursing a beer at a table off in the corner. Casey was drinking with a pal at the bar. The other man I know, by the way. I'd say there's no chance he would know what Casey'd been up to or they wouldn't've been drinking together. He's one of those real straight-laced New Englanders we get out here sometimes."

Longarm nodded. There would be time enough later to think about Pete Casey's drinking companions. In the meantime, Jamison's opinion seemed good enough.

92

"Anyhow, Casey hadn't been back in the camp more than a few hours. He'd got back from wherever he was that afternoon. I figured to keep my mouth shut and bide my time. Hadn't shown any interest in Pete and didn't intend to."

Again Longarm nodded. It was the same conclusion he had reached for his own planned surveillance of Bert Chambliss as soon as he showed up back in Leadville.

"Like I said, Casey'd only been here the afternoon and was having a drink or two. Not showing any great amount of cash, though he did pay for the first round with a gold eagle, which is usual around here. Mining men will only take their pay in gold coin. They're real funny about it.

"Casey and his companion were on about their third drink, neither of them loud or starting to show any sign of being drunk. Then these two bounty hunters came in."

"Broe and Moore?" Longarm asked.

"That's them, all right. I take it you know them?"

"We've met."

"I can just bet how well you like them two," said Jamison.

"How did they work it?"

"Real cute," the local deputy said. "They came in together, and there's no doubt but that they knew their man right off. Must have known he was in the saloon, even. They came in together but split apart as soon as they were inside. Broe was the one making a show of being there. He came straight up to the bar and stopped beside Casey. Nick Moore, he slipped around the wall of the tent and came up to the other side real soft-footed like. I doubt that Casey ever knew he was there. To tell you the truth, Marshal Long, I was watching Tyrone Broe too, and I never saw Moore pull his gun. I couldn't say exactly when he done that, but he sure had it ready in his hand when he wanted it.

"Anyhow, Broe stopped there beside Casey and gave him a hard looking over, enough to call attention to what he was doing. Casey noticed it too and asked what Broe was up to.

"Broe said he thought Casey looked like a man called Peter Casey, and Casey allowed as how that was who he was all right. Then Broe reached slow and careful inside his coat and pulled out a folded paper of some kind. I don't know if it was a legal paper or not, but Broe said it was. He told Casey it was a warrant for the arrest of Peter Casey on charges of train robbery."

Longarm shook his head. As far as he knew, no papers had been drawn up for the arrest of Casey or any of the other men. Deliberately. Once the warrants were issued they would have to be served, and Longarm wanted time to watch the men before they were picked up and put behind bars.

"Casey looked damn surprised, I'll tell you that. I was watching him, of course, and he went white in the face and did some cussing. He never reached for his gun, though. I'll swear to that. The only time his hand moved was to set his glass down on the bar.

"That's when Broe hollered something like 'Watch out for his gun!' and stepped to the side.

"And that damned Nick Moore shot Casey from behind. Shot him twice, right in the small of his back. Casey never had a chance. He went down and flopped around some and was dead inside of five minutes. Someone sent for the fellow he was sharing a cabin with up higher into the mountains—turned out to be his half-brother—but there wasn't time for him to get here before Casey was dead.

"We—uh—we're holding the body down in an old mine shaft where it's cool. In case you wanted to see him or something. As soon as you say it's all right, I'll release the body to this half-brother for the burying."

"You went through his personal effects to see if there was anything that could help us?"

"I did. There was some gold coin, which isn't identifiable so far as I know, and a pocket knife and a half-used plug of tobacco. That's about it. If what was in his pockets was his share of the train robbery loot, that was one helluva big gang, or else Pete Casey was a *real* big spender on his way back here, or else he stashed the rest of it somewhere. There wasn't but fourteen dollars in his pockets when he died."

Longarm cursed some before he said, "I can't think of any reason to go stare at a dead man I never met before. So far as I'm concerned, you can let the brother claim the body and save the county the expense of a burying. What about the reward on him?"

"I've already notified Ed Chapman, and I understand from him that the railroad is releasing the reward. Broe and Moore will collect that in Buena Vista, same as they did last time."

Longarm did some more highly creative cursing.

"Marshal?"

"Yeah?"

"I'm sorry. I am god-awful sorry that I couldn't do anything to stop those two. I'd've run them in myself for it, but what they did was technically legal as far as I can make out. If you know any different, I'd damn sure like to be the one to put the cuffs on them."

Longarm sighed. "No. You did exactly the same as I'd have done, Rick. There's nothing you should feel bad about, and nothing you could have done to change it. That's the pity of it. It was all legal. But now that's one less lead that we might have had toward whoever that bastard in the hood is."

He rubbed his grainy eyes, woefully aware that he had spent the previous night without a moment's rest on that bouncing stage. Now it looked like he would have to turn right around and head back for Leadville again.

When Bert Chambliss returned to the delectable Carrie's embraces, Longarm wanted to be there.

At least Ed Chapman had been right about one thing. Deputy Jamison was a good man.

Chapter 11

The stage connections from Blue Timber, high on the side of the Collegiates, to Leadville meant that Longarm would have to pass through Buena Vista and sit out a layover for the next northbound coach. It was a toss-up whether Longarm should try to catch a few minutes of uncomfortable sleep on a stage stop bench or check in with Ed Chapman. His sense of duty forced his tired pace in the direction of the sheriff's office.

"Hello, Ed, I . . . *you!*"

A grinning Tyrone Broe was seated in front of the sheriff's desk. There was no sign of Nick Moore.

"Fancy seeing you here again," Broe said. "Come to see how a better man than you gets *your* job done?"

"That will be the day," Longarm spat. He was bone-weary, irritable, and in no mood to fence with the likes of a greasy bounty hunter.

"Come to think of it, Broe, I've never seen any papers authorizing you to hunt men and collect bounties. I don't suppose you'd mind showing me something along that line."

Bounty hunters, contrary to popular belief, could not go into business for themselves on the basis of an arbitrary whim. In order for them to operate legally in any state or territory of the United States, they had to have official authorization from a court or a police agency. Some states, including Colorado, even required that such hunters of men be bonded.

If Broe was not able to produce any documentation, he could not collect the reward.

More to the point, if that happened to be the case Longarm would be able to arrest the son of a bitch and put him behind bars. It would not hold up for any great length of time, particularly since the railroad seemed to approve of Broe's results while not caring about his methods, but it might delay him long enough to put him out of the picture until Longarm could complete his investigation without further interference.

"You can show it to me, can't you?" Longarm demanded.

Broe was still grinning. "You're picking nits, Deputy."

"Maybe, but I'll see your damned papers or I'll slap some cuffs on you and haul you down to Denver for federal detention."

Broe turned his attention to Chapman, who still had not had a chance to speak, and said, "Sheriff, I want you to observe that my hand is not going anywhere near my gun now."

Chapman grunted.

With two fingers of his left hand, Broe gingerly pulled the lapel of his coat back so both law officers could see that he was not wearing an underarm rig. Carefully he used his other hand to dip into the inside coat pocket. He pulled out a thin leather wallet and flipped it toward Longarm.

The wallet held a single sheet of paper, yellowed with age and sweat and falling to pieces at the folds.

It was a handwritten statement from some jerkwater justice of the peace in a Nevada county deputizing Tyrone Broe and empowering him to arrest felons and/or serve warrants in the name of the J. P. The scrawled signature was illegible.

"I'm not so sure this will hold up, Mr. Broe. You don't mind if Sheriff Chapman checks it, do you?"

"I don't mind that at all, Deputy," Broe said. The bastard was still grinning. Longarm had not even succeeded in annoying him.

Which, Longarm thought, almost certainly proved that the damned J. P. would confirm the validity of the paper.

"In case you're wondering," Broe said, "Nick has a paper exactly like that one there." His grin became wider. "We're good citizens, you know. Cleanin' up this here country where the likes of you can't. We sure wouldn't want to go an' do anything that would be illegal."

Longarm refolded the paper, returned it to its case, and tossed it back to the bounty hunter.

"I was a nice try, Deputy, I'll give you that," Broe said comfortably.

"With that or without it, Broe, you're a murdering son of a bitch. And if you want to call me on that insult, I'm downright positive Sheriff Chapman there would testify that the survivor was shooting in self-defense."

"I think I would at that," Chapman said.

Broe laughed. "You can't bait me, Deputy. No way. I'm acting strictly within the law and within my own rights. There's not a damn thing you can do about it."

The unfortunate thing was that he was right.

"Has this piece of carrion gotten his thirty pieces of silver, Ed?" Longarm asked the sheriff.

Broe laughed. "A lot more than thirty pieces, Deputy, an' it's gold, not silver. The good sheriff here says it'll be delivered any time now."

Longarm turned and stalked out of the office. He had no right to throw a man out of someone else's office, but there was damn sure no requirement that Deputy Long breathe the same air as him. He could do the rest of his waiting at the stage stop, and the hell with Tyrone Broe. With any luck at all, Longarm would never have to see that son of a bitch again.

Longarm was walking down Leadville's Harrison Avenue toward State Street and the Beezle Bub when some fool behind him began shooting up the neighborhood. Gunshots in Leadville were common enough, but ahead, on State, not back in the business district, where they seemed to be coming from. Longarm was already in the protective cover of a store entrance with his Colt in his hand before he could consciously identify the source and direction of the noises.

He rubbed his burning eyes and wondered if it would be ethical for him to ignore whatever was going on back there and let the local law, what there was of it, take care of it.

He looked up and down the street. The local law did not seem to be in evidence at the moment. With a weary sigh he exposed an eyeball to the scene down Harrison.

One man, coatless and with his sleeves held up by garters, was lying on the sidewalk with a bright red pool staining the boards around him.

No trouble out of that fellow anymore, Longarm concluded.

Another man was still on his feet. This man, dressed in muddy overalls and a shapeless coat, was holding a Spencer carbine in his hands. He looked almost as pale as the dead or dying man he had just shot.

Longarm stepped cautiously into view—no one else seemed to be interested in taking a walk on the street at the moment—and walked slowly toward the man with the carbine. "Afternoon," he said politely.

The man with the carbine jumped. His knuckles went white as his grip tightened on the stock of the Spencer.

"Who are you?" The muzzle of the Spencer angled toward Longarm's belly.

Longarm smiled. "Right now, I'm a fella who wishes you'd point that thing somewhere else."

The man looked down at the carbine as though he had forgotten he was holding it. "Oh." But he did not move it aside.

"Mind telling me what this is all about?" Longarm inquired.

"Bastard tried to cheat me." He shot a nervous glance toward the much better dressed man who was bleeding to death.

No one, Longarm noticed, had yet come rushing to the fallen man's side to offer assistance. And Longarm did not think it was quite the moment for him to do so either.

"It isn't good to cheat people," Longarm said agreeably.

"Damn right it ain't."

"How did he do it?"

"Bankers. They're all alike, you know. Bunch of damn bloodsuckers. He tried to cheat me."

"Tell me about it." Longarm was painfully aware that the Spencer had been recocked and presumably therefore had had another round levered into the chamber. Unlike a Winchester, the war surplus Spencers had to be chambered and cocked separately. A throw of the short lever would not do both. So there was at least the possibility that the cocked hammer hung over an empty chamber. The likelihood seemed damn slim for a man to stake his life on it. And that gaping muzzle—.56 caliber? Longarm could not remember for sure—was still pointed waveringly toward Longarm's midsection.

"I come out here prospecting," the frightened man said. He licked his lips. "Found a likely place an' staked my claim. Ore black as a banker's heart an' rich with silver, but I needed money to get to it. Giant powder. Carts and rails. Things like that."

Longarm nodded. "I know how it is," he said soothingly.

"Right. So I borrowed from that son of a bitch over there. Developed my mine. It's payin' out just fine. Sell my ore to the Rose Brothers' smelter down there." He pointed with his chin in a direction that took in half the Leadville mining district. "Been paying off my note regular as could be. Installments, you know. Pay it off a bit at a time, each an' every month."

"I understand," Longarm said.

"Now this son of a bitch says I ain't made my payments. Pulls out a book to prove it. A damned *book*. I ask you, who do you think's been in charge of the book?"

"The banker?" Longarm guessed.

"Damn right it was that self-same son of a bitch. Been putting my money into his pocket each month, an' now that my mine's paying out he comes along and says I'm overdue on my note, so he can foreclose an' my mine will be his. Is that any kind of fair, I ask you?"

"Not hardly," Longarm agreed. "I—uh—don't suppose you saved your receipts for the payments?"

The man snorted. "Receipts. That's what them other fellers asked me about too. The son of a bitch never *gave* me no receipts. *I* knew I'd paid an' *he* knew I'd paid and I never thought to ask for some damned paper to prove what we *both* knowed I'd done."

"It sure sounds like he tried to cheat you," Longarm said. "But I reckon you got the best of him, at that. Unless I'm mistaken, I'd say that that rattle and gurgle over there was the sound of your banker closing out his books."

The man with the carbine smiled. "It sure did sound like that, didn't it?"

"You don't need that carbine anymore, do you?"

"What?"

"I will admit, neighbor, that you are making me somewhat nervous with that thing pointed at my gut."

"Oh." He looked down at it, his face once again registering surprise to find it there. He looked back at Longarm. "I ain't going to shoot you. You never tried to cheat me."

"No, and I would take it real kindly if you would point that thing in another direction and maybe let the hammer down so it'll be safe for folks in town here."

"Oh." The man seemed to puzzle over that for a moment. "Reckon I don't need it anymore, do I?"

"No, I'd say that you don't." Smiling pleasantly, Longarm holstered his Colt and stepped forward toward the man.

A look of sudden suspicion came over the man's face. The muzzle of the Spencer quit wavering and steadied on Longarm's belly. "Why'd you have your gun out like that? You fixing to shoot me?"

"Hell no," Longarm said. "I heard the shooting down here and didn't know what was going on. Now that I know, I put it away. I don't need it anymore than you need that carbine now. Isn't that right?"

"I dunno." The man bit at his underlip. "Seems I dunno much of anything anymore."

Smiling, Longarm took another step forward. He extended an empty hand. "Why don't you give me the Spencer now. The banker's dead. You don't need it."

The man looked down at it, confused.

"Please," Longarm said.

He took another step and was beside the man, inside the danger of the muzzle.

He laid one arm over the man's shoulders to comfort him and with his other hand gently detached the Spencer from the man's grasp. "There." He lowered the hammer to half cock and let the carbine drop into the dust of the street.

"D'you think it'll be all right now?" the man asked. His voice had taken on a thin, little-boy quality.

"I'm sure it will," Longarm soothed.

Within seconds the street was filled with milling, excited, loud-talking people, who must have been watching through the storefront windows. Men poured out of the bank building to gather in kneeling clusters beside the body of the dead man.

"Hang the son of a bitch!" one of the men from the bank shouted.

The cry was taken up by others in the street. They began to press in around Longarm and the confused and badly frightened killer. The recent gunman was trembling and pressed in closer to the protection of Longarm's comforting arm over his shoulders.

"We're not going to have any hanging here, boys," Longarm said quietly. We're just going to have a little talk with the gentleman here, and then a proper court of law will decide what happens after that. Do you understand me, boys?"

Longarm's gunmetal blue eyes locked on one of the loudest of the would-be hangmen. "You. Do you understand me?"

"Yes, sir."

A town constable in a bright blue jacket and baggy, unkempt trousers showed up finally at Longarm's side. "Who the hell are you?" he demanded.

Longarm showed him his badge. "I think we can discuss this better when this gentleman is out of the street and locked safely into a cell, don't you?"

"Who are you?" someone else demanded. He was a portly, well-dressed man in a charcoal gray business suit.

Longarm explained again.

The man grunted. "I'll tell you what, Marshal, I was watching through the bank window there after he shot poor Henry down in cold blood, and what you did here today was the coolest, bravest thing I have seen in a great while. A great while indeed. Your superiors will hear about this, Marshal."

"Thank you, sir, but what I'd really like for them to hear about would be a full investigation into the allegations of this gentleman here."

"I shall undertake that investigation personally, Marshal, I assure you. And I shall also be delighted to report your personal conduct to your superiors. I have friends in Washington, and they shall hear about it, I assure you."

Longarm forced a smile. He would just bet there would be a fair and impartial hearing into the poor, scared miner's allegations. There were times when even he wondered if there was such a thing as justice.

Still, it would run its course through the local law, and the law would be satisfied, and that would be the end of that. In the meantime, Custis Long had other fish to fry. He turned the frightened killer over to the town constable and resumed his interrupted journey toward the Beezle Bub. He wished he could get some sleep soon.

Chapter 12

Anna went onto her tiptoes to kiss the plump gentleman goodbye. Not a very discriminating fellow, Longarm noted; he allowed her to kiss him full on the lips. Then she turned and directed a brilliant smile toward Longarm.

"Where've you been, sweetie? I missed you so much." She captured his elbow in both of her hands and cuddled into his side with a kittenish wiggle. The girl seemed to have taken to her work with a will.

"Busy," Longarm answered.

"Well, you're back now, sweetie, an' that's what counts." She batted her eyelashes at him so outrageously, but in such complete seriousness, that it was all Longarm could do to keep himself from laughing. Surely there could not be men who would actually *believe* any of this.

He shook his head. On second thought, there must be.

"Something wrong, sweetie?"

"No," he said quickly. Damn it, he had work to do here. It wouldn't do to let his mind wander like that.

"I'm just awfully tired." He paused and added, "But I couldn't stay away from my pretty little redhead another minute."

Anna sighed happily. "You are *so* sweet."

"That's me," Longarm agreed.

"Do you want a drink now, or should we go right upstairs?"

"I'll let you decide, Anna, but if I have a drink now I'm likely to fall over sideways and start to snore."

Anna chuckled and pressed the firm mound of her crotch against his thigh. "Upstairs we go then, sweetie. You won't go to sleep there."

"Don't count on that." Every breath seemed to make Longarm feel more and more tired. Lack of sleep for too many hours, the disappointment of Pete Casey's death, the long and uncomfortable ride back to Leadville and now the come-down from an adreneline-charged surge of energy during that dust-up outside the bank; it was all too, too much. Longarm's feet were dragging.

"I'll help you," Anna said. The happy little whore tucked herself under his arm and actually tried to support some of his weight as they climbed the stairway toward the now familiar row of small rooms where the real business of the Beezle Bub took place.

Anna latched the door closed behind them and helped Longarm out of his clothing before she slipped off the thin chemise that was her working garb.

"You're just as pretty as I remembered," Longarm said, giving her the briefest of glances through bleary eyes. Anna smiled.

"What's your pleasure now, sweetie?" She pushed him flat against the bed.

Longarm's eyes drooped closed of their own volition, and his breathing began to slow. He could not at the moment remember if he had hung the holstered Colt .44 at the head of the bed. He knew that that should worry him, but at the moment it did not.

"I know what you'll like, sweetie." The voice seemed to reach him from some great, foggy distance.

There was a flutter of movement against bare flesh at his belly, and he could feel his cock being enveloped by something warm and wet. He was not sure what. He did not particularly care what.

Dim, faintly heard slurping sounds reached his ears. His breathing steadied into a slow, deep rhythm.

All sound and sensation seemed to float away from him.

Deputy United States Marshal Custis Long began to snore softly.

Longarm came awake with a snort and a violent spasm of sudden motion. His hand swept the Colt from its holster hanging near his head and he sat bolt upright in the strange bed. "Wha...?"

"It's all right, sweetie, it's all *right!*"

"Anna?" He rubbed his eyes and dropped the .44 back into its holster. "Sorry."

The sudden fear left the girl's face and she smiled. She finished closing the door behind her and latched it.

"Were you going out?" he asked.

Anna laughed. "I was coming back in, sweetie. You've been asleep for three hours. This is the fourth time I've come to see if you were awake yet."

"Damn." He must have been tired if she had been able to come and go like that. "Did we, uh...?" He was not sure how to continue that question.

Anna laughed again. "You sure did, sweetie, an' it was the slowest, sweetest, nicest flow I ever tasted. It just wouldn't quit comin'. Like to filled me up an' choked me, you did."

Longarm wondered if she was telling the truth or not. He could not remember, and probably never would know for sure.

"You want to go again, sweetie?"

He shook his head. "Let me wake up first."

"Sure." Anna seated herself beside him on the bed and trailed her fingertips across his belly and balls in a gentle caress. "In case you're wondering, I haven't touched any of your things. Your pockets are just the way you left them."

"I wasn't wondering," Longarm lied. "You're a good girl, Anna."

"Well, you're kinda special to me. Guess you always will be, you being my first an' everything." She smiled and bent to kiss him, considerately enough placing her lips at his ear instead of on his mouth.

"You're a good girl," he repeated.

She sat up and he reached for his vest. She anticipated his desire and handed him a cheroot and match from his tossed-aside clothing, held the match to light the cigar for him, and then tossed it aside. "By the way," she said when the tip was glowing satisfactorily, "your friend is downstairs."

"My friend?" He still felt a bit fuzzy and light-headed from the interrupted sleep.

"Carrie's boy friend. The one you were asking about before."

Chambliss! Longarm was wide awake now. "You say he's downstairs?"

Anna shrugged. "He was when I left to come up here."

"I'll have to speak to him after while," Longarm said, concealing from her the quickened interest he was feeling.

Longarm's intention right along had been to sit back and observe Bert Chambliss, hoping the outlaw would lead him to the hooded mastermind of the train-robbing gang. Now he was not so sure that that would be the best course of action.

With a pair of obviously well-informed and fast-shooting bounty hunters throwing wrenches into the works of this particular investigation, Longarm was wondering if he might be better off to slap a set of irons on Bert Chambliss and haul him down to Denver to join his former pal Tris Gay.

They would have the same leverage over Chambliss that they had over Gay—the prospect of a hanging for murder if they turned him over to the state authorities, or a jail sentence for train robbery if he agreed to co-operate with the federal investigation by naming the hooded man.

Longarm decided on the spur of the moment. Better to take the bastard alive and talking than risk having Chambliss also shot and silenced by Tyrone Broe and Nick Moore.

He stood and began to dress quickly, taking care to insure that the double action Colt was belted into exactly the right place at his left hip.

"Let's go down and have ourselves a drink, pretty Anna," he said, giving the girl a five-dollar half eagle for her troubles—whatever they might really have been. "And you can introduce me to Carrie's boy friend."

"Sure, sweetie." Her eyes were bright with pleasure at the size of her payment. She was undoubtedly over-joyed at the prospect of having more of the same from such a big spender who was so sweet on her. Longarm, on the other hand, was overjoyed at the the thought that he would not again have to employ the girl's none too clean services.

Carrie and Bert Chambliss were not in the parlor when Longarm and Anna got there, so Longarm took a seat in a corner of the room and let Anna bring him a glass of Maryland rye while he waited.

As usual there were more customers downstairs than there were girls available to service them, and Longarm noticed his redheaded sweetheart eyeing them nervously while she squirmed on the overstuffed arm of the chair he had chosen.

111

"I'm gonna be content with this glass of rye for a little while, Anna, if you have other things to do."

She grinned broadly. "You are *so* considerate, sweetie. That's what I just adore about you."

He noticed that her alleged adoration did not keep her from giving him a quick pat on the back of the neck, a quicker kiss on the ear, and trotting off to direct her smile at one of the prosperous-looking customers across the room. Within seconds the man had made a suggestion, Anna nodded a happy agreement, and the two were on their way up the staircase.

Such, Longarm thought, is the course of true love in a parlor house. Not that he was upset about it. Far from it. He took a swallow of the excellent rye she had brought him and pulled contentedly at his cheroot. He felt good about his decision to arrest Bert Chambliss now and try to convince him to share his information afterward.

Carrie came down the stairs several minutes later. The man with her was ordinary enough in appearance. He was of medium height and build, with black hair and a swooping mustache which was very much like Longarm's except for its darker color. He was the sort of man who would disappear in any crowd, probably an advantage in his line of work, Longarm thought. If he was carrying a weapon, it was hidden.

Of course he wouldn't be, Longarm remembered. He would have had to check it at the door. House rules.

But if that was so, why hadn't Miss Emmalene asked Longarm for his Colt this time? She always had taken it from him before, but not this visit. He had been so tired when he came in that the change in policy had not made any impression on him.

He shook his head, putting the question out of mind. Probably the old bat had forgotten, just as Longarm himself had. Right now he had other things to do—like have a word with Bert Chambliss.

Longarm drained off the last of the good Maryland

rye and set the glass aside. He ground his cheroot out in the ashtray beside his chair and stood.

"Chambliss."

There was no one between them. Most of the customers still downstairs were in the bar or were clustered around a spinet where one of the trollops was entertaining them while they waited.

Chambliss saw the tall, handsome deputy and blanched. The man's face went white around the black splash of mustache and dark eyes, and he stopped in mid-step at the bottom of the staircase.

"Easy now," Longarm said soothingly. "We need to have a talk, Bert."

The man's right hand twitched slightly, but Longarm did not react. Chambliss's coat was pulled back far enough by the angle of his shoulders for Longarm to see that there was no revolver on his hip.

"No trouble, Bert." Longarm began to walk forward slowly. He was ready for trouble, but he did not expect any. "We'll talk a little, all right?"

Chambliss licked his lips. He looked frightened. "You're the federal man was in that gunfight a while ago. I heard about that."

"That's right, Bert," Longarm said easily. "But you just stand easy now. We don't have to have any trouble here." He smiled. "No cause to get everyone upset when they've come in for an evening of relaxation an' pleasure." He was only a few paces away from Chambliss now.

Chambliss was paler than ever. A tic fluttered the corner of his left eye and he blinked rapidly as if he was trying to stop it.

Then, inexplicably, Chambliss relaxed.

Longarm could see the tension flow out of the man's body. The taut set of his shoulders loosened and the color returned to his face. He actually smiled. "Fuck off, federal man."

Longarm could not understand it.

Behind him a gun roared, the hollow boom of the explosion impossibly loud inside the confinement of the parlor walls, and Longarm saw a damp, red spot the size of a nickel appear above the bridge of Bert Chambliss's nose.

Before the echoing blast of gunfire died, Longarm was twisting and falling to the floor, his Colt in his hand and his eyes seeking a target.

He dropped, rolled, and came up on one knee with the .44 extended in front of him, his finger already applying the pressure that brought the double-action hammer back to full cock and rolled a fresh cartridge in line with the sightless barrel of the big Thunderer.

"Don't shoot, Marshal, it's us!"

Tyrone Broe and Nick Moore were standing in the doorway. Both men had their empty hands held out to their sides. A single-action Colt .45 lay on the rug at Broe's feet.

Barely in time Longarm released his trigger pressure and snapped the barrel of his .44 toward the ceiling.

"Don't by God move!" he ordered. He twisted his neck for a quick glance toward Bert Chambliss, but he need not have bothered.

The outlaw's body lay sprawled in an untidy heap at the foot of the stairs. Beside him Carrie was kneeling, already beginning to cry as she reached to cradle the shattered head of the man who had been one of her regulars.

Broe was grinning. "Reckon we saved your ass that time, Marshal," he said. "That son of a bitch carried a hideout gun, you know. He was going for it, an' woulda put a bullet into you if we hadn't taken him." The man let his arms fall to his sides and motioned for his partner to do the same. "Ain't that right, Nick?"

Moore nodded his agreement. "We both seen it. He was going for his hideout gun all right."

"That poor bastard was unarmed, and I had him under arrest," Longarm protested.

"Now, Marshal," Broe answered smoothly, "I never once heard you say a word 'bout arrest."

Broe retrieved his Colt Peacemaker from the floor, picking it up with only two fingers so there could be no doubt about what he was doing, and dropped it into his holster. "Check him, Nick."

Before Longarm could protest, Moore crossed the room to the dead man's side and knelt with his back to Longarm. He stood a moment later with a .41 caliber single-shot derringer in his hand. "See there, Marshal? Already had it in his palm, by damn. You'd've been a dead man, sure as shit, if Ty hadn't saved your life like he done."

Moore and Broe were both grinning.

"He was unarmed," Longarm insisted, but it sounded lame even to him.

"Right here's his gun, Marshal."

The other men in the room were crowding around the corpse now. One of them took the little derringer from Moore and examined it. "This thing's loaded, sure enough, Marshal," the man said.

Longarm shook his head. He was morally certain—damn well positive—that Bert Chambliss had been totally defenseless and unarmed when he came down those stairs. But with that derringer on display now, he knew good and well that these witnesses would testify about a derringer and not about an unarmed man when the inquest was held.

The derringer was a plant that Nick Moore had carried to the body with him. Longarm knew it. He also knew that he had no proof of it whatsoever. Neither he nor any of the roomful of witnesses had seen Moore make the plant.

Shit, Longarm thought with disgust.

"Ain't you gonna thank us for saving your life?" Broe asked with a wicked grin.

"What I ought to do is put you under arrest for obstructing justice," Longarm said bitterly.

"Why, sure, Marshal," Broe said with a laugh. "We'll go with you. Find you a judge an' tell him all the facts. 'Bout how we saved your life from that felon there who was about to gutshoot you. Sure thing. If you can convince a judge to issue you a warrant on that basis, why, Nick an' me will be happy to hold our wrists out for the cuffs. Won't we, Nick?"

Moore laughed. "Whatever you say, Ty."

Longarm bit back the rage that threatened to choke him. The worst part of it was, the son of a bitch was right. With the testimony of a whorehouse full of impartial witnesses to back their version of it, no judge anywhere would issue a warrant for the arrest of Tyrone Broe and Nick Moore. If anything, the judge would upbraid the federal deputy for being ungrateful.

Shit, he thought again. Right under his very nose. And he hadn't gotten around to actually saying the word "arrest" yet, so Broe and Moore could even claim the railroad's reward for Bert Chambliss's death.

He turned and stamped out of the Beezle Bub before his fury overcame his good judgment.

Those well-intentioned impartial witnesses would damn sure testify against him, federal badge or no federal badge, if he gave vent to the feelings he was experiencing toward those bounty hunters.

Chapter 13

"I want to hire a horse," Longarm told the liveryman.

The unshaven old hostler squinted at him and took his time about answering, first directing a stream of brown tobacco juice toward a rathole in the dirt floor of the stable. "Don't have much call for horses here."

"You have one now."

"Tough," the old man said.

"You don't have any horses at all?" Longarm asked incredulously.

"Nary a one," the liveryman agreed.

"Nothing a man can ride?"

"Didn't say that, did I? Said I don't have no horses."

"Then what the hell do you have?"

"Mules. Mules is what's called for up here."

"Saddle mules?"

The liveryman shrugged. "Got a couple that's said to be saddle broke. I don't guarantee 'em myself. Don't guarantee they got four legs apiece, though you're welcome to count for yourself. Welcome to hire 'em out

117

too. What you do with 'em afterward is your own affair."

Nice fellow, Longarm thought. "Trot one out then, old man."

The hostler spat and nodded. He took his time about it.

A good night's sleep had not done a whole hell of a lot for Longarm's sour disposition. Tyrone Broe and Nick Moore, he assumed, must be following him, letting Longarm lead them to the train robbers so they could step in, gun the quarry down, and collect rewards for their brave dead-or-alive captures.

It was a slick enough idea from their point of view, Longarm supposed, but it damn sure fouled up his investigation if he intended to reach the hooded man who was the gang leader.

And he damn sure intended to find that mysterious figure, if Broe and Moore could not eliminate all of his leads the way they had been doing so far.

Bastards, he thought once again wearily.

Still, if they were following him he might yet be able to give them the slip and concentrate his attention on the last gang member he had more or less spotted. Iceman Winter over in Fairplay.

Broe and Moore would probably have to go back to track's end in Buena Vista to collect their reward on the murdered Bert Chambliss. They would likely be expecting him to take the stage back there too, allowing them to file for their reward and keep an eye on the federal deputy at the same time.

Let them wait and watch down there all they wanted, Longarm thought. While they were in Buena Vista, Longarm would cut across Mosquito Pass to reach Fairplay and the Iceman.

The liveryman led an elderly, grizzled mule into the aisle of the barn. The animal had one ear that had been raggedly cropped short in some ancient encounter with

118

man or beast, and there were harness sores on its shoulders, showing that it had been badly used during its long lifetime. Longarm gave it a critical look and was not particularly encouraged by what he saw.

"You say that thing's saddle broke?" he asked.

"I don't say shit 'bout it myself," the old man told him. "I say that's what's been told to me. I'll tell you this much. The other un's even worse."

That hardly seemed possible, but Longarm decided to accept the old fellow's statement. "I'll try him, then."

"Suit yourself. I get my pay if you do or you don't."

I'll just bet you do, Longarm thought, but said nothing. He gave the man a voucher against the U. S. Treasury and threw his hornless McClellan saddle onto the old mule's back. He was mildly encouraged when the animal accepted the saddle with no sign of protest.

"Reckon I can loan you a crupper," the liveryman offered.

"Thanks." Longarm had a breaststrap with his saddle, but a riding mule, with no withers worth noticing, needs to have its saddle secured both front and rear to avoid having the saddle slide up and down the animal's back.

He finished tacking up the old mule and was pleased to find that it accepted his non-issue spade bit without protest. *So far so good,* he thought. *Now for the moment of truth.*

"Stand back, old man," he said. "I might be getting off in a bit of a hurry and I wouldn't want to step on you on the way down if that's the way she goes."

The liveryman grinned at him. He also stood well to the side.

Longarm cheeked the mule, pulling its nose back beside his left stirrup while he mounted and found a good, deep seat. He was more than half expecting a fight, and he had heard there was never a horse born that could match a mule when it came to bucking.

119

He took a deep breath and gave the mule its head.

The old beast just stood there with its one good ear cocked in Longarm's direction.

"I'll be damned."

Longarm touched his heel lightly to the mule's ribs, and the animal swung into a swift walk.

"I'll be double-dog damned."

He rode the mule around the livery stable, reined it in a figure-eight pattern, bumped it up to a high lope, and pulled it back into a hock-sliding stop. The old animal handled like a top-quality cowhorse.

"Son of a bitch," Longarm said when he returned to the stable. "I reckon you weren't lied to after all."

"Don't hardly believe it myself," the hostler said.

Longarm secured his Winchester beneath his right leg and tied his carpetbag behind the cantle, then remounted.

"Where'll you be taking the old bastard?" the livery-man asked.

"Dillon," Longarm lied. If anyone should ask—anyone like Tyrone Broe or Nick Moore in particular—there was no point in making things easier for them. "I'll bring him back by and by or else send him back."

"Makes no difference to me," the hostler said, "'less that voucher you gave me's no good."

"It's good unless the government's run out of money," Longarm said, "And if that happens we're all in so much trouble it won't matter nohow."

He rode north out of Leadville to reinforce the lie he had told about his direction, then doubled back and headed east up the long climb that would lead to Mosquito Pass and eventually to Fairplay in South Park on the other side of the Mosquito Range.

Chapter 14

The roadhouse below the crest of Mosquito Pass on the South Park side of the divide was an anthill of activity. Although much of the freight traffic for Leadville had already been diverted through Buena Vista and the longer but easier climb up the Arkansas River valley—and although the traffic would virtually disappear once the DSP&P reached Leadville in another year or two—there were still innumerable mule trains scurrying up and down the Mosquito Pass route, and the stage line was still active, dispatching four coaches in each direction daily as men and supplies poured into and out of the silver mining district.

The roadhouse was a two-story log structure surrounded by a swarm of mules, wagons, off-loaded pack-saddles, and three light coaches owned by the stage line, empty now, with their teams turned out of harness for the overnight stop. A good many men had built fires and were cooking their own suppers practically in the shadow of the stage stop.

Longarm unsaddled his hired mule, dumped his gear in a pile at the base of a Douglas fir, and tied the animal on a short picket line. A hostler who might have been a brother if not quite a twin of the liveryman back in Leadville sold him hay and grain for the mule.

"Supper's on the table inside if you don't want to do for yourself," the hostler told him.

Longarm nodded his thanks. Given a choice, he would take someone else's cooking—*anyone* else's cooking—in preference to his own.

"Your gear'll be safe enough here," the man said.

Longarm thanked him, but chose to carry his Winchester inside anyway. His faith in human nature only went so far.

The downstairs portion of the roadhouse was divided more or less equally into a restaurant on the right, where the entry was located, and a saloon in the left half. A stairway that was as much ladder as stairs led upward. A sign advertised bed space upstairs for fifteen cents.

The tables in the eating half of the place were all full, so Longarm drifted into the saloon section and found a place among the men lined up at the unpolished plank bar.

"What'll it be, neighbor?" The barman was busy but seemed unruffled by the commotion. He was undoubtedly used to dealing with crowds on a nightly basis, Longarm thought.

"Maryland rye," Longarm said hopefully.

The man grinned. "Try again."

"It was worth asking, anyway."

"What I got is keg whiskey for fifteen cents or bonded for a quarter. Take your pick."

Longarm fished in his pocket and laid a quarter on the bar. "I won't be wanting change."

"A wise choice. I know too much about the keg whiskey to drink it myself." He exchanged a filled glass for

122

the quarter and turned away to serve someone else.

Longarm took a swallow of the bonded whiskey and made a face. If the keg liquor was any worse than this, he was almighty glad he had made the choice he did.

"That bad, huh?"

Longarm turned to look. The man beside him at the bar was coatless and wore a leather vest and no garters on his shirt-sleeves. The drooping front of his wide-brimmed hat was pinned up with a long, wicked-looking thorn. He wore a Remington revolver carried high on his right hip, and deep sun creases fanned out from the corners of his eyes.

Longarm let his gaze drop down toward the man's booted feet. His boots were stitched with rows of bright yellow and red thread, and large roweled Mexican spurs dragged in the sawdust on the floor.

"Long way from Texas," Longarm observed.

"Ain't it just," the man agreed. He held a hand out to shake. "Billy B. Williams," the Texan said.

"Custis Long, but my friends call me Longarm." He accepted the offered hand.

"You ain't from Texas, Longarm."

"I've passed through."

"In which case you've been there long enough to be called a native," Williams said with a grin.

"Damn near," Longarm agreed.

Williams gave him a closer look. "You in cattle?"

"Not anymore."

"I'm glad to hear it."

Longarm raised an eyebrow.

The Texan grinned. "Competition. There ain't much up here the way things stand now, and until the railroad gets through there won't be much. A man can make a helluva profit trailing beef up here. Them miners like their meat an' taters as good as the next man. A man that knows what he's doing can buy beef cheap down in

123

the flatlands an' trail 'em up here for good money. Time the damn railroad puts me out of business I'll be a rich man."

"Then what?"

The Texan grinned even wider. "Go home to set in the shade and stay drunk. Get me a little Mex'can gal to fetch my whiskey an' keep my bed warm. Speakin' of whiskey, how 'bout another?"

"I could stand it."

They drank together and chatted until some of the crowd began to thin. Then they went in together to share a meal of venison stew in brown gravy, boiled potatoes, and slabs of crumbling cornbread.

"It ain't my idea of good," Billy B. said, "but it fills the empty in the gut."

"You've been here before?"

"Every time I take a herd up to sell. I'm on my way back down to the flatlands now."

"Where's your crew?" Williams seemed to be traveling alone, Longarm thought.

"Hell, I give up a long time ago trying to keep a crew together. Soon as they hit the high country they all get the notion they can walk out of town a ways an' fire a pistol in any direction, sure they'll hit a vein of gold or silver or maybe mother's milk. Happens every time. So I hire some boys one way and let 'em learn for themselves that there's no such thing as a free lunch. A man has to work for whatever he gets."

"That ain't always an easy lesson to learn," Longarm agreed.

He sopped up the last of his gravy with cornbread crumbs, spooned it into his mouth, and thought about another cup of coffee. He looked around for the pimply-faced waiter who had brought their meal.

"You won't get a refill if that's what you're wanting. They don't want anybody keeping the tables full after the meal's done and paid for. But I'll stand you another round in the saloon over there."

"Poor whiskey but good company," Longarm said.

Williams chuckled and led the way. They were no sooner out of their chairs than someone else was occupying them.

Williams ordered two glasses of the bonded and raised his in Longarm's direction. "To your good health, Longarm."

"And yours, Billy B."

"Say, you know all about me. What is it brings you up here?"

"Business."

"Which is?" the smiling Texan asked.

"I'm a deputy U. S. marshal, actually." Longarm smiled and took a sip of the inadequate whiskey.

He might as well have loosed a shotgun blast into the air from the reaction he got.

The Texan's smile froze into a rictus on his tanned face, and he became fish-belly white beneath the tan.

Williams let out a sharp, hissing sound and staggered backward a pace until he bumped into the man behind him at the bar.

"Gawd!" Williams moaned. "You son of a bitch. You set me up, didn't you?"

"I don't know what you mean, Billy," Longarm said. But he was afraid that he did understand, all too well. Somewhere, for some charge great or small, Billy B. Williams was a wanted man.

"You son of a bitch," Williams hissed.

"I'd sure prefer that you not say that, Billy. You're jumping to conclusions, old son. I don't know a thing on you." He sighed. "But now that you've brought it up I don't see any way I can ignore it, though I sure hell wish I could."

Williams was not listening to him, obviously. The

125

fear of iron bars and close confinement had closed his mind to everything else from the moment Longarm admitted his profession. "Bastard," he snarled.

"Damn it, Billy, I sure wish we hadn't got onto this conversation. Why don't we talk about it? Maybe the paper's been lifted on you, whatever it's about. I can check that for you by telegraph when we get down to Fairplay tomorrow."

The offer was as fair as Longarm knew how to make it. He meant it, too. He wished no harm to this friendly Texan and would gladly look for an excuse to let him go his own way.

Williams's mind was closed to the suggestion. He might not even have registered hearing it.

"You got to take me the hard way, you son of a bitch," he croaked.

Williams turned to square off with Longarm, and his right hand curled into a hook, ready to snatch at the gutta-percha grips of his revolver.

"You don't need to do that, Billy," Longarm said calmly. He was cursing inwardly, thinking that if Williams had not taken that involuntary step backward a moment ago he might be close enough for Longarm to grab his gun hand and get the handcuffs on him before any damage was done. As it was, though, he was just a bit too far out of reach for that to be a sensible alternative. "If you'll help me, damn it, maybe we can find a way out of this for you."

"You won't take me in, by God!" Williams declared in a voice that was on the thin edge of panic.

"Damn it, Billy!"

The tone of William's voice had cut through the many conversations around them, and now the room full of men was watching them. Those along the bar, the men behind Williams and Longarm alike, scattered like quail. Within seconds that section of the roadhouse was empty.

"Damn you!" William's voice was anguished.

He grabbed clumsily for the gunbutt in his holster, but the poor bastard was a cowman, not a gunfighter.

"Shit."

Longarm had no choice unless he wanted to stand there and be shot down by a man whose crimes he did not even know.

The big double-action Colt swept out, long practice bringing it in line with William's belly just as Longarm's finger tightened on the trigger, and the low-ceilinged saloon reverberated with the roar of a gunshot.

Longarm stepped swiftly aside, and Williams's gun came free of its leather. The Texan staggered and blinked. His vision seemed to be bad, and he was having trouble locating Longarm.

Behind Longarm there was the sound of stampeding boots as men threw themselves out of the line of fire.

"Don't, Billy," Longarm pleaded.

The Texan seemed to locate him by sound, and turned the muzzle of his Remington that way.

Longarm shot into him again, a bitter taste rising in his throat that had nothing to do with the acrid stench of burnt black powder in close quarters.

Williams's knees buckled and he went to the floor. His gun fell from his nerveless fingers and dropped with a dull plop into the sawdust.

Longarm knelt beside the man, but it was plain that there was nothing he could do for him now. His eyes were already glassy and his lips were pale.

"You won't take me," Williams whispered.

"No, Billy, I won't ever take you in," Longarm said gently.

He picked up the fallen Remington and tossed it aside, then stood and reached for his wallet and badge before any of the other customers might mistake what had just taken place.

Son of a bitch, Longarm told himself.

He didn't even know what Billy B. Williams had been

127

wanted for, and he might never know.

It was, Longarm thought, *one hell of a waste*.

"Easy boys," he said loudly, getting control of himself. "I'm a federal marshal. It's all over now."

Several other men slipped immediately out of the room and made tracks for the front door. Longarm did not even want to know why they were leaving.

Chapter 15

"Are you all right?" he asked with concern. The answer was all too obvious.

Jane gave him a wan smile and a shrug. There was no way she could have hidden the purple and yellow discolorations on the left side of her face that were the fading remains of what must have been extraordinarily ugly bruises there.

Longarm's plan was backfiring. He had come here hoping to be cheered up by the friendship of this gentle woman. After the disappointments of the investigation and the waste of the Texan's death, he had felt in need of some cheerful companionship to take his mind off things.

Now, looking at what MacRae had done to Jane, he was angrier than ever.

"Is Donny all right?" he asked.

"A little sore, but . . ." She did not finish.

They were sitting at her kitchen table. Donny was playing somewhere with his friends. MacRae apparently

129

was at work. Longarm had no desire to inflict harm on innocent men, but at the moment the thought of a mine-shaft accident would not have displeased him. Not if Brent MacRae was in the shaft at the time.

"What happened?"

Jane shrugged again. "Brent got it in mind that..." She looked away. "He accused me of taking a lover, Custis."

"Unfaithful? You? That's insane, Janie."

Jane MacRae was as good and decent and as fine a woman as Longarm had ever known or hoped to know. The idea of her doing anything remotely improper was beyond comprehension. The idea of her doing anything that was actually immoral was utterly impossible. She was Longarm's idea of what decent womankind should be and, once in a very great while, could be. He could not imagine a woman of her quality violating her marriage vows.

"I know, Custis, but Brent has it in mind that...that you and I..."

"*Me?* You and me? My God, Janie!"

"Please don't say anything, Custis. It would only make things worse."

Longarm clenched his fists and ground his teeth together in an effort to keep his mouth shut. MacRae had gone entirely too far in his wild imaginings, by damn.

Not only was Jane MacRae too good and decent a woman for her to ever be unfaithful to her vows, now the bastard was accusing Longarm of violating the purity of one of the few women he held so dear as to be far, far beyond any desires of the flesh. She was a friend and the wife of a friend—the widow of one, in any event—and he would rather lose his manhood than dishonor her with it. He had never even *thought* about her in carnal terms, and now for that damned Brent to *accuse* her... He shook his head with mingled anguish and anger.

130

"Oh, Janie, what can I do?" he asked sadly.

"Nothing, Custis. Nothing at all, I'm afraid."

"Wouldn't you please let me send you back to your family? The train could have you back with them in practically no time. And Lord knows there are some judges who owe me some favors. You could get a divorce from MacRae. Better yet, an annulment. It could be very quiet. No one back there would ever have to know about it."

Her smile was very sad. "I would know, Custis."

He sighed. "Is there nothing, then?"

"There is one thing."

"Of course."

"Remain my friend?"

"Always. I hope you know that. Yours and Donny's too."

"That means a very great deal to both of us, Custis."

"But . . ."

"No. Nothing more than that. I stood before God and joined my life with Brent's. I'll not try to pretend that never happened." She gave him a small smile. "And really, it isn't all that bad. It comes and goes. I'm learning to be careful, and to keep Donny out of his way. We will be all right, believe me."

"All right, but if there is ever anything I can do . . ."

"If there is, I will come to you. I promise."

Longarm nodded, and realized that he should leave this house as quickly as possible now.

He wanted to keep out of sight in Fairplay just as much as he possibly could, both to keep from spooking Iceman Winter and to keep Broe and Moore from realizing where he was. Hell, he had even had some thoughts about asking if he could hole up in the MacRae house while he waited for the Iceman to surface. But with Brent MacRae acting like such a suspicious fool, he could not make matters worse for poor Jane by making that request.

131

He stood. "I'd better go now," he said, "before someone sees me here and mentions it to that idiot you're married to."

"I hate to say it, Custis, but you could be right."

"If you need me, I . . ." He thought quickly. "I probably will be staying clear of the hotels. I may be able to work it out so I can rent bed space in a Chinaman's shack at the northeast edge of town. You might be able to find me there, or get word to me anyway." He described the shack for her.

"I know it. The laundry girl lives there, I believe."

Longarm nodded. He thought he felt his ears redden slightly, but he tried to ignore that and hoped Jane did not notice.

Whether she did or not, if she thought anything about the impropriety of a handsome single man taking a bed in the shack of an unmarried Celestial, she said nothing.

"If there is anything at all—" he repeated.

"I know." She hurried him toward the back door. "You are a dear friend, Custis. Thank you for that."

Longarm went on his way with a heavy heart.

Longarm hesitated for a moment before he knocked on Chen Li's door. The way his luck was running lately, there would already be someone there with her and he would have to slink away like a schoolboy rejected by the town tramp.

Not that he intended to draw any comparison between that kind of woman and Chen Li. She seemed to be a fine little woman caught up in a harsh way of life.

Li answered his knock and he was reminded once again, of just how very little she was. It was not exactly so, of course, but she gave the impression of coming little higher than his belt buckle when she stood in front of him.

"Long Custis!" She greeted him with a pleased smile. "Welcome."

He swept off his snuff-brown Stetson and held it politely before him. "You—uh—are alone, Li?"

"Yes, very, until the joy of your visit." She stepped aside and motioned for him to come in.

It was about time something went the way he wanted it to, Longarm thought.

Li bowed to him and said, "My home is yours, Long Custis."

Longarm smiled. "You just can't know what a pleasure it is to hear you say that."

She looked puzzled. "You would explain, please?"

He did. When he was done, Li smiled. "I would be honored to help a friend who has done so much for me."

"If you're sure it wouldn't put you out to..."

"Please." She cut him short. "I would truly be honored. And you should know that there is little which happens in any town that is unknown to its servants. There are others like me here. A few more. And some servants with black skin. We see and hear very much, but we are not seen. The good people of the town—any town, not only this one—pass us in the street, even in their own homes. Their feet move to avoid us but their eyes do not see us. We are not really there, eh?"

Longarm nodded. He was an observant man himself, but even so he tended to look beyond the cleaning girl in a hotel hallway. It was something a person did without thinking. It was also something that might be put to good use from time to time.

"If this man is in the town," Li said, "I will know about it very soon."

"You wouldn't mind?"

"No more of such talk," she insisted. "It is a small thing I can do for you." She smiled. "With luck, there will be another thing I might do for you, Long Custis."

He grinned, correctly guessing her meaning, and pulled the tiny woman to him.

He had to lift her off her feet to kiss her, but the small

133

amount of work was well worthwhile. She tasted fresh and clean, and her tongue probed delightfully inside his mouth. The contrast between this delightful little Oriental and the slut back in Leadville was extreme. He found it a relief to be holding Chen Li.

Longarm cradled her in his powerful arms and continued to kiss her while her deft fingers went about the business of unbuttoning him.

"Set me down, please. I cannot reach all the buttons from here."

He did as she asked, and she knelt to tug free the buckle of his gunbelt and open his fly. It took him very little time indeed to undress, and Li was only seconds behind him.

Longarm picked her up again and placed her gently on the narrow bed in her shack. He lay on top of her and enjoyed the feel of her skin, cool and satin-smooth, against his.

She seemed as anxious as he was, and pulled him over her. Longarm allowed her to guide him inside her. She was not fully wet yet and he had difficulty entering. Twice he tried to stop, to give her time to be ready to receive his great size, but both times her fingers insisted that he continue.

"Ahhhh!" she moaned softly as he slid full-length into her tiny body. "Yes, my long, long Custis."

Longarm stroked slowly in and out, giving her time to accept his size. He was in no hurry, and wanted her to have an opportunity for pleasure too.

He could feel a decided difference as her passion rose and she became more and more moist and ready. He slid easily in and out, his pubic hair grinding against her almost hairless mound, and his hips bearing down on her high, arched pelvic bones as he thrust into her, the tip of him barely contained within her tight grasp with every withdrawal.

Li's breath began to quicken, and he could feel the

rise and fall of her hips as she strove to meet his strokes. She wrapped her arms tightly around him, and he could feel her nails biting into his back.

"My long, long Custis," she said happily into the hair on his chest.

He speeded the rhythm of his strokes slightly, and Li responded at once with rapid movement and ragged breathing.

"Now!" she cried out. "Please!"

Longarm pulled back, paused for half an instant and rammed himself harshly forward. Li's breath caught in her throat.

He began bucking and plunging, holding himself back but thrusting harder and faster while Li squirmed and strained to hold more and more of him inside her.

She arched her back and clung to him fiercely with her arms and legs, and the strength that was in that tiny body was amazing.

She threw her head back and cried out aloud, and her small, vibrant body became for a moment as taut as a strong bow as she reached her climax with a shuddering intensity.

Longarm made one final, impossibly deep thrust into the warm depths of her and held himself there while, impaled, she quivered and wept and clung to him.

"Did I hurt you?" he asked, with genuine concern. For those last moments he had forgotten how very small she was, and he could have injured her.

Li wrapped her arms around him again, more gently this time, and laughed with joy. "Hurt me? Oh, no, Long Custis. You give me great happiness, but never hurt."

"You're sure?"

"Yes, very." She sighed and let her lovely little body go limp beneath him. "Oh, *very*"

Longarm smiled. He had to reach so far down to kiss her that he very nearly slipped out of her from the contortions that were required.

Li's eyes widened. "But you are still hard, Long Custis."

He grinned at her. "Uh-huh. I'm having a good time. Don't want it to come to an end too soon, you know."

Li smiled and wriggled out from under him. "I believe I know a way, Long Custis, that will turn a minute into an hour and make you sure that the mountains will crumble before the next daylight. You are willing?" She knelt on the edge of the bed beside him, tiny and lovely, and damned if she didn't manage to look modest, even though she was delightfully naked, with a sheen of moisture between her slim thighs.

"I expect I would be willing," Longarm said.

"Then please, Long Custis, lie on your back with your eyes closed. Put all thoughts of every kind away from your mind. And allow me the honor of giving you pleasure."

Longarm grinned and did as he was asked.

"You weren't gone long," he said groggily when Li returned. Her attentions had taken only an hour out of his afternoon, but when she was done he had had to look out the window twice to convince himself that it was not—as he certainly felt it should have been—the middle of the night. He felt like he could have slept the clock around with no effort at all, and as it was he had been dozing while she was out.

"There was not so many to speak to," Li said. "I have asked about this man called Iceman."

"And?"

She shook her head. "He is not here. Not at this moment. But the black-skinned girl who is called Sadie, and who works at the hotel near the courthouse, says that she knows the man. She says he stays often in a cabin near Mosquito Gulch and comes to the hotel to drink and to visit with a man who sometimes stays at the hotel."

Longarm had ridden through Mosquito Gulch on his way back to Fairplay. The road to Mosquito Pass ran through it and the less used road beyond to Alma and Hoosier Pass.

"He isn't here now, though?"

"Sadie will tell me when he returns."

Longarm nodded. That was fine. Much more interesting, though, was the idea that Charles Winter had been visiting with a guest at the hotel. It seemed at least possible that the man Winter met there was the mysterious hooded gent who was so clever about robbing trains.

"Does Sadie know anything about the man Iceman met at the hotel?"

"I did not ask her this. I did not think of your needs. Please forgive me, Long Custis." Chen Li acted as if she had completely failed him. She looked ashamed.

"Goodness, Li, I didn't ask you to. You couldn't have known."

"I will go now and ask her about the second man."

"It would be a lot of bother—" He was already talking to an empty room.

Li was back within ten minutes. "She does not know the second man, although she has seen him."

Longarm nodded. Even so, it was better than he could have expected. He could go over there and take a look at the guest register. That would mean letting more people know he was in town, but it should be worth it.

Li pulled a bundle from under her shift. "Sadie said you may know him. He was in room 121 two weeks ago Wednesday and Thursday also. She does not know how to read, but she believes you may be able to find the information you wish from this book."

Son of a bitch, Longarm thought. The two of them had somehow stolen the register for him.

His excitement growing, Longarm flipped the book open and counted back the correct number of days.

"Damn," he muttered, and let it fall shut. The room

had been signed for by John Smith.

"I guess we can think of *some* way to fill in the time until Sadie says the Iceman has come back," Longarm said.

Li laughed. "That may be possible, Long Custis, yes. There must be a way to fill the time."

She slipped her shift over her head and let it fall to the floor at her feet.

Chapter 16

"The one called Iceman is at the Three Nuggets saloon," Li said with excitement as she closed the door behind her. "Sadie found me and told me this not two minutes ago."

Longarm smiled. He had been holed up in Chen Li's shack for two days now, and by this time he was seriously out of touch with Billy Vail. Vail was probably going to be angry. But it looked as though the waiting and the hiding had paid off.

"What about the other man?" Longarm asked. "The one he met here before."

"Sadie said this Mr. Smith is not at the hotel, but she has seen a man in town who could have been the same one."

Longarm grinned and checked to make sure his Colt was riding precisely where he wanted it for a quick fast draw and that his hideout derringer was secure in his vest pocket. He looked at the Winchester standing in a corner of Li's shack, but decided against the encumbrance of the longer weapon. If Charles Winter offered a fight it would be in the close quarters of a barroom, where a rifle is more handicap than asset. Besides, Longarm's intention was to take the man very much alive and able to talk.

The possibility that the hooded "John Smith" might also be in town and available for capture added to the zest of the moment. Longarm felt strongly that Smith was the ultimate target of this investigation.

"You will please be careful, Long Custis?" Li asked.

"Of course," he told her with a smile and a kiss. "Just doing my job, you know."

"Now I know what it is to be frightened for you."

Longarm ignored her concern. She was a nice gal, sure, but at the moment he had other things to think about.

The Three Nuggets, built by a man who had purchased his initial stock in trade with the proceeds from three large gold nuggets taken from Tarryall Creek and who had never once looked back toward the uncertainties of placer mining since that time, was only a block and a half away. Longarm loosened the Colt in his holster as he walked toward the saloon with long, sure strides.

As he had intended to do with Bert Chambliss, he wanted to take Iceman Winter alive. With any luck at all a little verbal persuasion—like pointing out the difference between iron bars and a hangman's noose—would prompt the man to peach on his boss.

And once Longarm knew John Smith's actual identity, the case would be as good as closed.

He strode easily to the door of the Three Nuggets and swung the batwing doors aside. He was already beginning to feel the relaxation that came with the end of a job. And that proved to be a mistake.

He almost walked into the back of a man standing squared off inside the door of the saloon, facing another man who was a stranger to Longarm.

The man who was turned away from him had his hat tipped back on his head, so the only thing Longarm could see of him was the brim of his Stetson and a few straggly curls of unkempt hair. The man Longarm could see was poised with his hand over the butt of a revolver jammed into his waistband.

The fool who would butt into the middle of someone else's fight was a double-damn fool, and Custis Long had no particular desire to be listed in that category.

Saloon brawls with firearms were common enough in mining camps. Their usual result was that the men would empty their guns at each other and then be so nervous they could not reload to try it again. Amazingly often, each man would fire a full cylinder of cartridges in the general direction of the other, yet neither would be hurt when the smoke cleared. On the other hand, a stray bullet cares not a bit who or what it strikes. Longarm slipped quickly to the side, well out of the line of fire, in case these two midday drunks got up the nerve to have at each other.

The man standing beside the bar was a rough-looking customer, and seemed more than willing to use the gun that was in his waistband. He was ruggedly handsome except for some pitting on his face from a bout of pox at some time in the past. His clothes were travel-stained, and he looked damn well able to take care of himself. He was the kind that, given a choice, Longarm would always prefer to take quietly and from behind. At the moment he looked like a man who had been backed into a corner and was willing and able to fight his way out of it.

"I won't take shit from any man," he snarled at the man whose back was to Longarm. "So you turn your ass around and crawl out of here or die, mister. It don't make no never-mind to me which it is. Shoot or crawl, mister. An' if you shoot, you die."

Longarm took another precautionary step backward until he reached the wall. Then he crabbed sideways along it away from the combatants.

He had no idea what any of this was about, but he had no desire to speak up or ask questions until the two men were in a mood to listen. Now that they were keyed up to a high pitch of nerves and murderous intent, it was entirely too likely that a word spoken by a stranger would set them both into motion. And there was sure the possibility that they might shoot at the man who spoke and not the one who faced them. No, *later* would be the time to act official and wave badges and foolishness like that. Right now, Longarm was getting the hell out of the way.

"Well?" the man by the bar demanded.

There was no response from the other one.

"Turn and crawl, cocksucker."

There was a flicker of motion at a side door of the saloon, and the man at the bar cut his eyes toward it for an instant. His eyes widened in surprise, possibly at the realization that he had made a terrible mistake, and the other man's hand dipped toward his own gun.

The man at the bar was good. Longarm had to give him credit for that. He knew he was behind by at least half a heartbeat, but his hand flashed toward the butt of his revolver, and he had it out and talking before the other man.

He put his first bullet into the chest of the man who was facing him.

But spears of lead and flame were coming at him from two directions now. From the man he faced and from the side door too.

The man was caught in a crossfire and must have known he was as good as dead, but he took the lead and braced himself with his feet wide while the noise and stink of gunsmoke filled the room.

He took his time about deliberately cocking and aiming his revolver with hands that could have had no strength, and he sighted carefully before he fired again into the forehead of the man who was facing him.

The other man's hat flew off, and the underside of it was covered with a glistening sheen of bright red moisture. He crumpled to the floor. For the first time Longarm got a look at the second man.

Son of a damned old bitch, he told himself. The second man was Nick Moore.

Which logically meant that the man by the bar, who was sinking to his knees now, was Iceman Winter.

Ed Chapman had said the Iceman was a tough customer. By damn, he was.

He was already more dead than dying, but still he did not quit. He hit the floor but somehow retained his hold on his revolver. He raised himself on one elbow and used both hands to try to recock the weapon while the son of a bitch at the side door took aim for a finishing shot. He stepped forward and raised his gun and Longarm could see that it was Tyrone Broe.

"Halt in the name of the law!" Longarm shouted into the noise and the confusion of the scene. He felt silly saying it, but at the moment he could not think of anything better to yell.

Both Broe and Winter ignored him, if they heard him at all. Winter was trying with all his failing strength to bring his gun muzzle to bear on Broe's belly. And Broe was taking careful aim at the Iceman's head.

"Stop!" Longarm hollered helplessly. He began to run forward.

Broe's revolver spat flame, and a halo of pink and gray spray hung for a moment around Charles Winter's shattered head.

Longarm stopped. His Colt was out and pointed at the bounty hunter's belly, and his finger was already tightening on the double-action trigger when he realized what he was doing and released the pressure at the last moment.

Broe looked up at him. He registered no surprise at all. Instead he grinned broadly and with slow movements reached out to lay his gun on the surface of the bar beside him.

"Good," he said with satisfaction. "You were here to see it then. He wouldn't come, so we had no choice but to take the bastard dead."

Broe glanced with little interest toward his late partner's body, saw that Moore was dead, and bent to begin going through Winter's pockets.

"You will turn those personal effects in with a full accounting, I assume," Longarm said.

Broe looked up at him and grinned. "Of course, Deputy. Wouldn't dream of doing otherwise. As a matter of fact, you're welcome to take over here now. I'd consider it a favor. Also if you was to testify that I took this man right an' proper within the law."

Longarm felt disgust rising in his gorge like vomit. He looked at the Colt still in his hand and jammed it back into his holster before the temptation to use it became overwhelming. He had just seen murder done again, and he sorely wanted to see justice done, for a change.

Longarm wished that, just this once, he could forget that the law was no good if the men who were supposed to enforce it abused it instead. Just this once.

He gave Tyrone Broe a glare of raw hatred and turned away. He had to get the hell out of that saloon or he would shoot the son of a bitch in cold blood.

Chapter 17

"You're down to one last name on your list of suspects," Sheriff Ed Chapman remarked.

"Don't I know it," Longarm said. The evening train had brought him to Buena Vista in search of understanding companionship more than anything else, if the truth were known. Now he and Chapman were slumped into easy chairs in the sheriff's home with a bottle of Maryland rye between them. The excellent whiskey was doing nothing to lift Longarm's spirits.

"I don't suppose your boys have heard anything about the last gang member?" Longarm asked.

"Not a word."

"Teale, wasn't it?"

Chapman nodded. "Ben Teale. Benny to his friends. Just a kid, the way I hear it, probably like that boy you have in jail down in Denver. My deputies have been doing a lot of asking about him. They're learning everything except where he is now."

Longarm leaned back against the cushions of the chair,

closed his eyes, and took a deep swallow of the whiskey. He thought about lighting a cheroot but rejected it. For one thing, he would have to stir enough to reach into his pocket for one. For another, maybe a dose of self-discipline would be good for him at this point. The way things were going lately, he could begin to feel almighty useless.

"Benny came out here from Connecticut," Chapman droned on. "He wanted to make his fortune by picking up free money out of the streambeds, but he didn't want to get his feet wet doing it. He worked off and on as a mucker for one mine or another, gambled some, drank whenever he had the money or could find a sucker for a hard-luck story. Wasn't much account to start with and didn't get any better.

"He was known to associate with Peter Casey, which probably explains his recruitment into the gang."

"Nothing there about a John Smith?" Longarm asked. "Who is John Smith?"

Longarm explained, including his gut feeling that Smith was the hooded mystery man they wanted.

"Hell, Longarm, I've known two dozen men who are actually named John Smith. That's why the damn name works as an alias. It really is common."

"I know, damn it, but I have this feeling . . ." He could not explain it any better than that.

"All right. I've had those feelings myself from time to time. I reckon every good lawman does."

Longarm snorted. "If you're talking about good lawmen," he said with disgust, "maybe you'd better leave me out of the discussion, Ed. I ain't showing myself so damn proud lately."

"I don't believe I've ever heard anyone claim that this job was easy," Chapman said softly. "Not anyone, at least, who knew anything about it. For damn sure no one who's ever carried a badge."

"Tyrone Broe seems to find it easy enough."

146

It was Ed Chapman's turn to snort. "If you're setting up to model yourself after Tyrone Broe, Deputy, then I'm gonna wire my old friend Billy Vail and ask him to fire your ass for the good of the federal government."

Longarm took another swallow of the rye. He also said the hell with self-control, sat up, and lighted a cheroot. "Your boys haven't seen Benny, huh?"

"Not a smell of him," Chapman confirmed.

"Jesus, Ed, I feel like I'm at a dead end."

"Sleep on it, Longarm. Maybe something will come to you."

"Sure," Longarm said bitterly. "Maybe in the morning Benny Teale will knock on your door and ask would you please arrest him and take his confession and oh, by the way, here's the name and the location of the ringleader."

Chapman was grinning, and Longarm found himself smiling back at the man in spite of himself.

"Go upstairs," Chapman told him. "There's an empty bed in the guest room, and you can carry that bottle along with you. We'll talk again come morning."

Longarm nodded and levered himself upright out of the depths of the comfortable chair. "Maybe you're right. Hell, things can't get any worse, can they?"

Chapman laughed. "I wouldn't tempt fate that way if I were you, Longarm. Say that things can't get worse, an' usually they do."

In the morning Longarm was smiling and scratching. He joked his way through the ham and biscuits and redeye gravy Ed Chapman's wife prepared for them and was in a good humor when he walked with the sheriff to his office.

"I'm going to have to pay more attention to that rye whiskey you favor," Chapman observed. "It sure seems to put a smile on a sad man's face."

"You said it yourself, Ed—sleeping on things sometimes gives a body an idea. Well, I've got me an idea about who this Mr. John Smith is."

"Who?"

Longarm shook his head. "I'm not positive yet, but at least I have a thought on the subject. Don't really want to say anything until I can figure a way to smoke him out of the bushes. For which I got *no* ideas yet. But something will come to me, I'm sure of that."

"All right."

"There's a favor you could do for me if you would," Longarm said.

"Name it."

"Could you have your boys put the word out, quiet-like and kind of on the side so it won't be known where the word comes from, that this Benny Teale has been spotted?"

"Hell, yes, they could do that. Easiest thing in the world."

Longarm grinned. "Have them spread it around that Teale's going to be seeing a girl friend in Fairplay."

"In Fairplay? The sheriff there doesn't like you worth a shit, friend. If you're putting out bait, which I have to assume you are, you could do it as easily around here, where my boys can give you a hand."

"I know that, Ed, and I appreciate it. But, well, there's a personal reason why I'd rather hang close over there. A lady I might be able to convince she needs my help. I don't like the idea of letting personal problems interfere with my work. But, hell, if I'm spreading bait with lies anyway it can as easily be there as here."

Again Chapman accepted his judgment without any questions. "That's good enough for me." If he suspected that Longarm merely wanted to be shacked up with a girl friend himself—and Longarm could not have blamed him for thinking so—he made no mention of it.

Now, Longarm thought, he only had to figure out one minor thing. How the *hell* was he going to trap John Smith into revealing himself?

The best he could come up with would be to plant more bait for Mr. John Smith in the form of a rumored, but untrue, large shipment of payroll coins to one of the mines near Fairplay.

The bait Ed Chapman was spreading about Benny Teale should keep Smith in the vicinity, intending to silence the last gang member, until the other plan could take effect.

Then, if Longarm was incredibly dumb-lucky, maybe Smith would participate himself in a heist of the supposed payroll shipment.

More likely the wily bastard would just recruit another gang to do his work. Longarm questioned the ethics of a peace officer deliberately enticing a criminal into further crime, but he simply could think of no other way to get Smith to expose himself.

In the meantime, he nosed around Fairplay, Garo, and Red Hill Station, asking innocuous questions from time to time and keeping his eyes and ears wide open.

He was tempted more than once to call at the MacRae home to see how Jane and Donny were getting along, but he didn't dare. His presence there could only cause trouble for them if Brent MacRae found out about it. He had to be content with sending Jane a note by way of Chen Li, whose presence as the town's laundress no one questioned, letting Jane know that he was there if or when she would accept his help.

Since it would have been impossible to keep his presence a secret and still ask the questions he needed answered, he checked into the hotel and moved freely on the streets this time.

The primary drawback was that Tyrone Broe was still in town also. Broe had received his reward money for the capture—dead rather than alive—of Charles Winter, and now seemed to be cooling his heels in comfort.

No wonder, Longarm thought. This time Broe didn't even have to split the reward with Nick Moore. The bastard certainly did not seem to have been devastated by the loss of his partner. He spent his time drinking and screwing, and all too often his path and Longarm's crossed in the small town.

Thursday night Longarm received a disquieting telegram from Billy Vail.

It was unlike the chief marshal to issue arbitrary orders, but the telegram said only:

REPORT DENVER OFFICE IMMEDIATELY COMMA IN PERSON STOP

Curious, and also wondering if he was in for a dressing-down from his chief because the gang was virtually eliminated while Longarm continued his work on the case, he took the next train down.

When he returned to Fairplay that same night, Deputy Marshal Long was whistling and did not at all give the appearance of a man whose ass was sore from a chewing.

Chapter 18

"Yes, ma'am, Charles Winter was his name. He's dead now; killed down in Fairplay. What I'm looking for is a friend of his who sometimes went by the name of Smith. John Smith."

"I know Charles, of course. Knew him, that is. I rent out those cabins you see in the trees back there. He stayed there off and on with Hank Lewis."

"Yes, ma'am," Longarm said. That much he already knew. It was the reason he had come up to Mosquito Gulch.

"The other gentleman you asked about, though, I don't know," she said. She smiled. "There are a good many Smiths in these mountains, Marshal, but I don't recall any of them being friendly with Charles."

The woman, apparently landlady to quite a few of the miners in the Alma district, was an odd duck in some way that Longarm could not quite put his finger to.

She was probably in her mid-thirties, and there was nothing feminine about her. She wore her hair cut short

151

and was dressed in ragged trousers and a man's shirt, but there was nothing exceptional about that in a country where a woman alone would have to fend for herself. She had introduced herself, quite firmly, as *Miss* McKittrick, and if she had had a part in the construction of all those rented cabins she would have to be a capable woman indeed.

She wore no powder or rouge, of course, and under the loose fit of the shapeless shirt she wore it was impossible to tell anything about her figure—assuming she had one.

Still, there was something about Miss McKittrick that was slightly out of place. It nagged at Longarm because he could not identify it.

Not that it was any of his business, he reminded himself. Just his natural curiosity, which was one of the personal quirks that most really good lawmen seemed to have. He was always curious about what made people tick.

"What about this Hank Lewis, ma'am?" he asked.

She shrugged. "I don't know much about the man except that he pays his rent on time each and every month. He came out here from Ohio. I think he mentioned to me that Charles did too. At least I got that impression somewhere. I could be mistaken."

"Lewis is still using your cabin then, ma'am?"

"Oh, yes. He's working day shift. He gets off at four and usually comes straight home to clean up before he goes anywhere for the evening."

"Would it be all right if I waited here for him, then?"

"Certainly, Marshal. But I would prefer you wait at Hank's cabin rather than here. I have to drive in to town for some groceries, and I prefer not to have anyone in my place when I'm away." She gave him a smile that just missed being sincere. "Not that I would suspect a United States marshal, but . . ."

152

"I understand, ma'am. Don't blame you a bit. Which is Hank Lewis's cabin?"

She pointed it out, and Longarm rode the few hundred yards to it on the horse he had rented for the day. The grizzled mule he had ridden to Leadville had been long since sent back to its owner.

Lewis's door was unlocked, but this was hardly the empty lonesome back country where a man could be expected to make himself welcome under another man's roof without invitation. So Longarm dragged a billet of split wood up against the front wall of the log structure and settled himself on it in the sunshine.

The day was pleasantly warm, in spite of the altitude, and if Longarm was not careful he might even find himself adjusting to the thinness of the high mountain air. Certainly he was not bothered nearly so much now as he had been before.

He tugged his hat low over his eyes, leaned back against the peeling bark of the logs, and lighted a cheroot.

Across the meadow that sloped toward the bottom of the shallow depression that was Mosquito Gulch, he could see Miss McKittrick leaving her home. It was also a log cabin, but somewhat more substantial than her rental cabins. She checked to insure that the door was locked. Her buggy horse had to be harnessed and hitched before she could leave, but she was as competent as any man in the everyday chore, he noted. He wondered if he should have gone over there and offered to hitch the horse for her, then decided that she would be as likely to resent the offer as to appreciate it.

When Miss McKittrick drove out of sight there were only some flies and, far overhead, a loafing eagle to keep him company.

Longarm felt his head nodding from time to time as the sun warmed him and a deep, peaceful silence surrounded him. On an impulse he removed his coat and

153

let the sun bake through his shirt and vest.

He was drowsing and might have drifted off to sleep when a flicker of movement caught his eye and brought him awake.

The motion, he was sure, had come from the McKittrick cabin. And there was not supposed to be anyone around the house when Miss McKittrick was away.

Longarm remained still, the angle of his head unchanged, but his eyes were alert and probing under the lowered brim of his Stetson.

There. He saw it again, and this time there was no doubt. The movement was *inside* the cabin. He could definitely see something pale, a shirt perhaps, moving beyond the glass of one of the windows in Miss McKittrick's place.

Son of a bitch, Longarm thought. Who'd have guessed there would be a prowler prowling in such peaceful surroundings?

Longarm stood, pushed his hat back where it belonged, and ambled across the meadow toward the cabin. If the burglar had any sense at all, he would be keeping an eye out through the window, so pretty soon Longarm could expect to see the slinking son bolt out the front door. With just that in mind, Longarm hefted his Winchester in his hand and stood ready to use it.

He reached the house without seeing or hearing any burglar run, which was only mildly surprising. When you got to expecting sensible reactions from a thief you were making wild assumptions, because any halfway sensible person is not going to turn to thievery.

Careful to keep out of any direct line of fire from the few windows, Longarm circled the cabin the long way around to reach the front door. He could see no sign of forced entry.

There was also, though, no sign of entry at the front door. A padlock hung secure in a hasp where Miss McKittrick had locked it. Probably, he thought, the burglar had jimmied a window to get in.

Trapped yourself right proper, Longarm silently told the thief. He walked around to the window on the opposite side of the cabin where he had been sitting—the only logical place the thief could have entered—and tried to push it open.

Locked. Damn. It looked as if the burglar had locked it behind him. Probably saw Longarm nosing around outside and, not knowing he was a lawman, simply locked the window himself to make it seem like everything was in order. *Won't work,* Longarm told the silent burglar. He tried the window again, more forcefully this time.

It still held and, hoping to avoid the necessity of breaking one of Miss McKittrick's windows, he walked around toward the front of the cabin again, intending to try another window there.

As he reached the front of the place he heard an unmistakable squeal of fear from inside the cabin. And it was a woman's voice.

Longarm's reaction was immediate. There was a woman in there, and she was in danger. Without stopping to think, he snatched his Colt from his holster, shattered the padlock with one quick bullet, and threw himself against the door.

The damn door wasn't latched, though, and it offered no resistance to his battering weight. The door swung easily inward, and Deputy Long fell headlong through the empty gap with his arms flailing and his legs unable to keep pace with his racing body.

He hit the floor with a thump and slid across the planks, picking up a dandy collection of splinters as he went. The woman screamed again.

Longarm thrashed around trying to regain his feet, but something had his legs entangled as effectively as a fish in a net.

He flung himself sideways, female screams ringing in his ears, and he tried to find a target.

"Leave her be, goddammit!" he yelled. "I'm coming, lady, I'm coming!"

He gathered his legs under him for another attempt to stand, realized with disgust that it was a throw rug that had thrown him, and kicked the handwoven rag rug aside. "I'm coming, lady," he hollered again.

The woman screamed, louder than ever this time.

She was in another room ahead and to the right of where he stood, behind a closed door. Longarm scrambled to his feet and charged forward.

This time he gave the door a shove with his hand before he threw himself against it. The precaution was unnecessary. The door was locked and latched. Longarm took a few paces backward and threw himself against the wooden door.

It hurt like hell, but the wood splintered and he could feel it begin to give.

"Hurt her, you son of a bitch, and you'll face federal charges," he growled at the closed door. He had no idea what federal charges could possibly apply there, but then the burglar could probably supply some with his own imagination. This was no time to fret about details. "I'm coming, lady!"

He flung himself against the door again, and this time there was a loud crack and the solid door split into two sagging pieces that hung in the doorframe.

Now, by God."

Colt in his hand and fury in his heart, Longarm kicked aside the last lingering splinters of door and leaped into the opening.

He came to an almost immediate halt, the Colt's muzzle drooping and confusion in his eyes.

Lady?

"Lady?" Longarm repeated.

She screamed, a high-pitched, wailing sound of sheer terror.

"Lady? Please! Where is he?" If she heard him, the sound of his voice only served to intensify her fear, for her screaming became all the louder and more prolonged.

Longarm looked around in utter confusion. He was pretty sure—he ducked his head and looked under the bed, then he *was* sure—that this woman and he were the only two people in the room.

So where was the burglar? Quickly he crossed the room to the window. The window was shut and the sash locked. It was completely apparent that the frightened, screaming woman in the bed had not let any burglar out and then locked the window behind him.

"Lady, please!" At the moment all he could see of her was a mass of blonde curls showing above a bedsheet that had been pulled up head-high. He couldn't *see* much of her, but he was having no trouble *hearing* her.

Longarm took the few additional steps necessary to reach the bed from the window and bent over to try to comfort her. "It's all right, lady. He's gone now. Whoever he was, he's gone now."

The screaming slowed, quavered onward for another moment or two, and then stopped. Longarm was grateful for that. As it was, he thought his hearing might have been permanently damaged.

"Lady?" he said softly.

The tautly held sheet moved slightly, and Longarm could see the edge of one china-blue eye peering out.

Unfortunately that eyeball came to light immediately beside the Colt that Longarm still held forgotten in his hand.

The woman began to scream again.

Longarm's patience was quite used up. He rammed the revolver back into its holster and took a firm grip on the edge of the sheet. *"Shut up!"* he snarled. It worked.

"Now come out from under there and tell me what's going on here," Longarm ordered. He yanked the sheet

157

angrily aside, telling her, "Damn it, lady, I'm a deputy United States marshal. and...*Jeez!*" He snatched the sheet back where it had been, jumped to attention, and spun to put his back to her, all in practically the same motion.

The woman was naked. Completely, totally, and actually quite fetchingly naked. Beautiful was the correct word for it. She had a body that was...Longarm got some measure of control of himself. She had a body that was unclothed, that was what she had, and here he was standing in her bedroom with the locked door in splinters.

"I'm sorry, lady, I didn't know. But where's the damned intruder, lady?"

"What?" It was the first word she had said. Hardly the first sound he had heard out of her, but certainly the first word.

"The burglar. The thief. Whatever. I heard you screaming and figured you needed help. That's why I came busting in here like that. So where's the intruder?"

It was her turn to sound puzzled. *"You're* the intruder."

"Ma'am?"

"You're the reason I screamed. I saw you trying to break in through the window. Then I heard you out front. I thought if Hattie hadn't locked the door..."

"But I...Oh, Lordy." Without thinking, Longarm sat heavily on the side of the bed. The woman squirmed away as far as the double bed would permit her to go, her sheet clutched to her bosom—a nicely swelling bosom—and fresh panic in her eyes.

Longarm jumped bolt upright again. "No, lady, it's all right." He twisted his head and squinted at her. "There was nobody here until I came busting in?"

She nodded.

"And Hattie, that'd be Miss McKittrick?"

She nodded.

"Miss McKittrick told me there wouldn't be anybody

around while she was gone."

"No one is supposed to know I'm here."

Longarm accepted that. It wasn't any of his business, and it looked as if he had done quite enough already that was well beyond the scope of his business here.

"So when I saw someone—you, I expect now—moving around inside here, I figured someone had come in and was robbing Miss McKittrick. So I came over to catch him in the act. Except it looks like there wasn't anybody to catch but me." He looked sheepish.

The woman at least had a sense of humor. Her eyes— that was about all he could see of her at the moment— crinkled prettily, and could hear her chuckle. "You haven't come to rape me, then?"

"No, ma'am," he said with heartfelt sincerity.

"And you really are a marshal?"

"Yes, ma'am." He produced his badge and held it out for her inspection.

"Deputy Marshal Long, is it?"

"Yes, ma'am, although my friends call me Longarm."

"Could I ask you a favor, Marshal Long?"

"Ma'am, I would have serious difficulty refusing you *any* kind of favor after this blunder."

"In that case, Marshal, would you please leave my bedroom while I dress? I'll be out in a minute."

He was out of the bedroom within seconds, thought about stopping to try to do something about the somewhat shredded condition of the bedroom door, reconsidered, and got the hell out of sight as quickly as possible.

The woman was as good as her word. She was dressed and in the main room of the cabin very quickly.

Now that he could get a look at her without the glare from his bright red cheeks interfering with his vision, Longarm could see that the blonde woman was about as pretty a piece of femininity as he had seen in a long, long while.

Pale blonde hair, bright blue eyes, and facial features

that were sheer perfection. She had a fine-boned delicacy reminiscent of exquisite porcelain, and her skin was utterly flawless. Her lips were a moistly inviting red and her face had a cool, powdered look that most women would have sold their souls to possess. Apart from her beauty, which was stunning, she had an aura of smoldering sensuality about her that made Longarm itch in a most unseemly manner.

Her dress matched her appearance, a confection of lace and silk in pale, shimmering colors. Longarm had no idea how much a gown like that would cost, but he suspected that its price would feed a family for a hell of a long time.

Yet she carried herself with complete disregard for her beauty or for the impact she must surely have on any man. The sensuality that surrounded her was simply a part of her, and she seemed to be unaware of it. Certainly there was no posing or artifice about her.

Longarm hoped that he would be able to get out of the front door without stepping on his tongue.

"You said you would be willing to do me a favor, Marshal?"

"Certainly. Dang near anything, at this point."

"I do have one to ask of you. As I mentioned already, no one is supposed to know that I am here. I have—well—no desire to be found by my former husband. And it would be very difficult, for me and for Hattie, if he were to discover me here."

"I can promise you no one will hear about if from me, ma'am," Longarm said solemnly.

"Thank you, Marshal." She smiled, and Longarm had to clamp his jaws shut to keep his throat from turning inside out.

"It would distress me terribly if I were responsible for ruining dear Hattie's reputation."

"Yes, ma'am."

"And now, Marshal, if you would allow me my privacy?"

"Yes, ma'am." Longarm floated out the front door like a sleepwalker. He found his Winchester where he had dropped it outside and walked back toward Hank Lewis's rented cabin.

He was halfway there before he started to groan and gnash his teeth. Just a little. With regret.

He had gone that far before he realized two things: It was Miss Hattie McKittrick's *reputation* that beautiful creature was worried about preserving. *And there was only one bed in Miss Hattie McKittrick's cabin.*

Custis Long had never, ever before been jealous of a dumpy, mannish female of the species.

He damn sure was jealous of Miss Hattie McKittrick.

Chapter 19

Longarm sat in his hotel room with a telegraph message crumpled in his fist, grinding his teeth and cursing to himself. Lewis had not returned to his cabin, and Longarm had given up on that slim lead for now.

He knew the contents of the message by heart after four readings, and if there was a loophole he could somehow wriggle through he damn sure could not find it.

CEASE PREPARATIONS STOP U S ATTORNEY DISALLOWS PLAN STOP DANGER TO CIVILIANS BEYOND SCOPE OF ETHICAL STANDARDS STOP WILL CONSIDER ALTERNATIVES STOP

The telegram was signed William—not Billy, *William*—Vail. There was no question that he would be given any leeway on the decision if Vail was being that formal about it, and Longarm knew it.

Son of a bitch, he told himself. His idea about setting

Smith up with a phony payroll shipment had been rejected by the U. S. Attorney. Too much danger to innocents who would be riding the train. And even if they had been able to talk the railroad into running a special train with no civilian passengers aboard, as Longarm had argued, the DSP&P crew would have to be aboard. There was no way he could have claimed that *they* would not have been endangered by the planned robbery.

Not that Longarm could really blame the man for his decision.

Longarm had wrestled with the idea himself on precisely those same grounds.

But, damn it, he could not think of any other way to force Smith into the open.

He shook his head angrily. The big, rotten, ugly, glaring "if" here was that if he could not come up with a sensible alternative, Mr. John Smith would be able to retire in comfort, and no one would be able to touch a hair on the slimy bastard's head. The idea of Smith walking away scot free was repugnant enough to make even Billy Vail's best deputy marshal want to go out and get stinking drunk.

He stood and shrugged into his coat, intending to go downstairs to the saloon and see just how drunk he could get before noon. He was interrupted by the sound of footsteps in the hallway beyond his door and a light, tentative rap of knuckles against the wood.

When he opened the door, Jane MacRae was standing there. The left side of her face was swollen and beginning to color, and there was a drying trace of blood around her mouth and beneath her nose. Her dress, a housedress obviously not intended to be seen on the public streets, was torn at the sleeves and bodice and showed more signs of drying blood.

She was crying in great, gulping sobs, and seemed on the verge of hysteria. "I need...I need...I need help, Custis. God forgive me, I need help."

Jane collapsed into his arms as he reached for her. She was out cold when he picked her up, kicked the hotel room door shut behind him with his heel, and hurried with her to the bed.

He grabbed the pitcher of water from its stand near the window and dropped into it the flimsy excuse for a towel the hotel provided to its guests. Worry and anger creased Longarm's forehead as, very gently, he began to bathe her battered face with the cool, cleansing water.

When Jane finally came around again, she began babbling so rapidly she was incoherent. Longarm waited her out, letting her get it out of her system. The poor woman had taken a terrible beating. If there was this much injury that he could see, she must be horribly battered on the rest of her body also, although it would take the assistance of another woman to look her over and give any aid there.

Brent MacRae was going to pay for this, one way or another, Longarm swore, if it took his own resignation and a fast gun to do it. The son of a bitch was not going to harm a friend of his and get away with it.

Jane's babbling began to stutter to a halt. Deciding she might be able now to speak coherently, Longarm said, "Donny, Jane. Where's Donny?"

A slight alteration in her expression showed that she had heard him, even though she was not yet willing to look him in the eyes.

"Is he all right, Janie?"

She turned her head away, but she nodded. The motion seemed to require that a price be paid in the coin of harsh pain.

Longarm reached for his nearly empty traveling bottle of Maryland rye. He did not have a clean glass in the room, so he shoved the mouth of the bottle under her nose, let her smell of it so she would know what it was and then held it for her to drink from.

"More?" she asked. It was a good sign, he thought. He gave her several more short swallows before she motioned the bottle away.

"Is Donny all right?" he asked again, now that she seemed in better control.

"I sent him away," she whispered. "He isn't badly hurt. I made him run. I made him run from Brent. That...that's what made Brent so angry this time. I made Donny run." Bright tears oozed from the corners of her eyes and ran down her discolored cheeks.

"I need your help, Custis."

"I know, Janie. I know that." He used the damp cloth to bathe her face as soothingly as he knew how. "I'll get you tickets to home. I'll buy them. No one needs to know who uses them. And I have a little money of my own with me. It isn't much, but it will be enough to get you back to your own people." He continued to stroke her forehead with the soothing cloth.

Jane MacRae squeezed her eyes shut, and the tears began to run more freely. "You don't understand, Custis."

"I do, Janie. I do understand. And I'm going to help you. I promise you that. I'm going to help you."

She shook her head so violently that his hand was flung aside. "You don't understand," she insisted.

"All right. Tell me." He had dealt often enough before with people who insisted that other people did not understand their problems. Sometimes they were right, too. The only way to find out was to listen.

"I can't...I can't...can't go home now." She was sobbing harder than ever.

"Why, Jane?" he asked softly.

"I can't...I can't...Custis?"

"Yes, Janie."

"Would you please be the one to arrest me? I don't want...don't want any of these deputies here to arrest

166

me. They were all so friendly with Brent and . . . I couldn't stand the thought of one of them arresting me."

"Arrest you, Janie? Whatever for?"

"I thought . . . I thought I told you." Her eyes widened and her voice became a moaning wail. "I've killed him, Custis. I've killed Brent MacRae, *and I'm glad I did*."

Janie had gone into a spasm of grief and fear and anger so intense that Longarm had not been able to rouse her from it. Nor was he sure that he should. Crying it all out might well be the best thing for her. In the meantime, he decided, he had better determine if she had been telling him the truth.

He could not leave her alone in her condition, so he went swiftly to his window and leaned out of the second-floor room to hail a boy on the street. He gave the child a message to deliver and tossed him a coin.

In less than five minutes, Chen Li was there.

"Poor little missy," Chen Li said with sympathetic concern.

"I'd like you to take care of her while I'm gone, Li."

"Of course, Long Custis."

"And while I'm gone, maybe you should check for any injuries in places that a man shouldn't look."

"Yes." Chen Li paused. "Long Custis, will you go to find the man who did this to the little missy?"

"Yes."

"Then hurry, go. I will watch over the missy here." She hustled him out of the door with barely enough time to grab his hat and his Winchester.

Longarm made a point of keeping his pace to a normal walk as he went to the MacRae home. If Jane was right about believing she had killed Brent MacRae, he would deal with it. If she was wrong, well, he would deal with that, too. There was no need to alert all of Fairplay that something was wrong at the MacRae house, either way.

The front door was closed and locked, but the back door was standing open. Longarm let himself in without knocking.

The scene he found in the kitchen where once he had sat drinking coffee with a dear lady was enough to take away any urgency he might have been feeling.

Brent MacRae was sprawled on the kitchen floor like so much cold clay. A cane with a heavy brass knob lay near the door into the dining room. Beside MacRae was a cast-iron skillet almost as large as those used by trail cooks.

There was not much question about whether MacRae was dead. His forehead had been flattened and rearranged to an ugly, unnatural slope.

A skillet, it seemed, could do just as good a job as a Colt.

Habit led Longarm to kneel beside the dead man and feel for a pulse, but there was none, and there never would be again. He rocked back on his heels and let his breath out in a low whistle. When she finally decided to get riled, Janie had herself quite a temper.

Since there seemed to be no reason now to be in a hurry, Longarm helped himself to a chair at the table beside MacRae's body and made himself free with a cup of the coffee that was still on the stove. She must have been starting lunch when the dust-up started.

Time to do some thinking before he did any acting, he decided. He sat there for the better part of half an hour, drinking the coffee and smoking while he did some ruminating about how this should be handled.

Murder was a bad thing, of course, but the presence of that cane and Brent MacRae's past history of wife- and child-beating took him out of the running for Longarm's sympathies. It was self-defense, plain and simple.

And, he realized, a coroner's inquest, particularly in a town where law enforcement was as much by whim as by writ and where the dearly departed was a good ol' drinking buddy of the local law—well, at the very best the inquest would leave ugly scars that would be carried by Jane and Donny for the rest of their days.

Assuming, of course, that the lady was formally charged with the death of her late husband.

Longarm began to smile. He lighted another cheroot and clenched it between his teeth, wiggling it up and down while he grinned and grinned.

When he was done congratulating himself, the deputy stirred around and began to make a few minor adjustments to the scene of the crime.

He picked the cane up and replaced it in the brass umbrella stand near the front door. *Oops,* he thought, *no more proof of self-defense. Sorry 'bout that.*

He picked up the iron skillet, amazed by how heavy the damn thing was, and used some of Janie's household water supply to wash it before he replaced it, after a search, in the proper cabinet with the other cooking utensils. *Golly gee,* he thought, *now there ain't even a murder weapon in view.*

He picked Brent MacRae up, with some difficulty, and propped the gentleman in the kitchen chair Longarm himself had recently vacated. Had MacRae smoked cigars too? Longarm could not remember at the moment. What the hell. He put the saucer he had used as an ashtray by the dead man's hand and tucked one of his own half-smoked cheroots between MacRae's cold fingers. *Now we don't even have a victim,* he told himself with satisfaction.

Finally, whistling happily, the federal deputy very carefully positioned a lamp on the sideboard, checked to make sure there was plenty of coal oil in the reservoir, and lighted it. It was not quite yet noon. Longarm adjusted the wick to a fine, butterfly glow and nodded happily.

A tidy domestic scene, he thought with satisfaction.

Longarm let himself out the back door of the MacRae

house and made his way at a casual pace back to the hotel.

Concealing a felony was something of a felony itself, wasn't it? He was sure it was.

He grinned wickedly around the stub of a cheroot.

"Everything is going to be all right," Longarm said reassuringly. He took another look at Jane, propped against his pillows on the hotel bed. Between them she and Chen Li had made her marginally presentable. Enough for travel, anyway. Everyone inevitably looked rumpled and unclean after enough hours of travel.

"I talked to Brent, Janie."

Her eyes widened with shock, and Longarm held a hand up to stop the flow of questions he knew she was about to ask.

"It's all right. Just listen to me."

She nodded. She looked reluctant, but she nodded.

"You didn't kill him, Janie. He's mad as hell, I'll give you that, and he has an awful goose-egg on his head. Prob'ly won't be able to wear a hat comfortably for a couple of weeks." Longarm chuckled. "He said you cracked him with a skillet? Personally, I think a meat cleaver would have been better, but I guess it turned out better this way.

"Like I said, he's sore as hell. In more than one way. He doesn't want to see you or Donny, neither one, ever again. I took the liberty of telling him I reckoned that would be just fine by you too. Was that all right?"

Relief at what she was hearing had brought her back to the verge of tears again, but she was able to nod.

"Good. I figured it would be." Longarm sighed. "I can't say that Brent is a real forgiving man, Janie. He doesn't want you to set foot in that house again, or he'll have you charged with assault and maybe half a dozen other excuses to make you miserable. Even so, I figure if you can walk away with the clothes on your back and a train ticket in your pocket, well, you're ahead of the game.

"So I kinda promised that you won't ever go to the house again." He fished a folder of papers from his inside coat pocket and handed them to her.

"I stopped at the stage office on my way here. Here's two tickets for the stage, one for you and one for Donny. And—" he reached into his pocket again—"here's some cash. Lord knows it ain't much, maybe not even enough, but it will have to do."

Jane accepted the tickets and the money wordlessly. She seemed to be numbed, in a state of shock. That was pretty reasonable, Longarm thought, for someone who had just learned that she had not committed murder.

"If you can tell Chen Li where you sent Donny, I'll bet she'd be willing to ge fetch him back here. Then the two of you can get on the next stage down to Garo and the next train down to Denver an' to all the wide, wonderful points beyond."

She smiled. "I . . . don't know what to say, Custis."

"You don't have to say anything. Hell, Janie, one of the better things friends are for is helping out when there's need for it. You or Charlie would've done just as much for me if the positions were reversed, and you and I both know it. Maybe the day'll come when I'll need your help or that of that fine son of yours. Comes that time, why, I'll ask. And I'm betting you'll give it."

"Of *course* we would, Custis."

"Hush now. And I'm really sorry that I can't stay here to see you off, but maybe Chen Li will continue to give you a hand." He paused to look at the Chinese woman, and received the nod from her that he had expected. He winked at her before he went on. "I have work to do. Official type work, so I don't have any choice about it. I hope you'll understand and accept my apologies."

He managed to give the impression that he considered himself to be deserting her in her hour of need, and, as he had hoped, Jane quickly forgave him.

"Good, then. I have to hurry now, Janie, so give Donny a hug and, if he ain't too man-tall yet, a kiss from his Uncle Cuss. Write to me and let me know when you're settled."

"I will," she promised. She even managed a small smile. "And I'm sure Donny isn't too grown up to accept a kiss from you."

"All right, then." He bent and gave Janie a quick peck on the less bruised of her swollen cheeks. "I have to go now."

For a half-assed sort of felon, Longarm was feeling pretty pleased with himself when he let himself out of the hotel room and headed for the livery stable.

He wanted to get a move on because, while he more or less knew which direction he needed to take, he had never yet been over the route.

Come to think of it, he realized as he walked, it had been Brent MacRae who told him the way.

Chapter 20

Longarm tied the rented horse to the nearest post, glared at it once, and took an extra few moments to hobble the ornery creature as well. It was a balky creature and he knew better than to trust it. Apparently it felt just as fondly toward him, because it tried to add Longarm's left ear to its diet when he knelt to apply the hobbles. He punched the horse in the muzzle and told it, "What I think I'm gonna do with you, old son, is buy you off that liveryman back in Fairplay. Then I'm gonna hire a special coach of the DSP&P to haul you down to Denver. Then I'm gonna curry and groom you and ride out to the edge of the city. And *then,* you cantankerous son of a bitch, I'm gonna sell you for *glue* and buy a bottle of it my own self just so's I can laugh every time I need something glued. You got that?"

The horse snorted, blowing several globs of snot onto Longarm's coat-sleeve. He was more than half sure the damned animal had done it on purpose.

Still, he was not here for pleasantries. He looked to

make sure he was in the right place, although he pretty much had to be. The sign hanging over the rail station platform said it was Red Hill Station. That was another way of saying it was a pimple on the butt of South Park. Practically unused nowadays, but ideal for what Longarm wanted to do.

The Red Hill station clerk must have felt much the same way about his duty post. He looked actually relieved to see a live human being to break the monotony of whatever it was he did here.

"Yes, sir, can I help you, sir?" He looked positively eager to be of service.

"I'd like to send a telegram," Longarm said. "I can do that here, can't I?"

"Absolutely, sir. You can send a message here to practically anyplace in these United States. We aren't the big outfit, but we sure have a tie-in to their lines. Greatest boon to mankind since the invention of women," the clerk said with a grin.

"Then I expect you could send a message from here to Fairplay?" Longarm asked.

The clerk looked confused. "Sir?"

"I can send a message from here to Fairplay, can't I?"

"Yes, sir, but . . . you know, don't you, that Fairplay's just four miles across those hills there?"

"I know, but this is official government business, and I have to be making tracks in another direction."

"Oh." The man nodded his understanding. He also tried to look more serious and self-important now that he was going to be handling official government business. He picked up his message pad and pencil.

"Send it to Deputy United States Marshal Custis Long," he said, "care of the county sheriff, Fairplay, Colorado. You got that?"

"Yes, sir. Absolutely."

"Good." Longarm pulled a cheroot from his pocket

174

and lighted it. He leaned back against the wall of the tiny rail station and composed his telegram as he went along.

It would have been better, all things considered, if he had been able to transmit the message himself, but he was not sure of the identification codes used by the DSP&P operators. And he did want to make sure his message was properly delivered.

"Got that?" he asked when he was done.

"Absolutely, sir." The clerk read back what he had written on his pad.

"Perfect," Longarm said with satisfaction. He paid the man, using some of his own money he had reluctantly held back when he gave Jane her traveling funds, and went out to reclaim the wonderful beast the Fairplay livery had wished off on him.

No doubt they let out that horse at every opportunity, Longarm felt, in the fond hope that some poor soul was not going to be able to control himself and would shoot the thing. Then he would have to pay for its replacement. If he hadn't given most of his own money to Jane, he just might have done it himself.

He glanced at the afternoon sun and grinned. Plenty of time yet. Plenty of time to ride wide around Fairplay and hide the horse in a place where, with any luck, it would fall down and break its fool neck. And do a little waiting.

Uh-huh, he thought. *Plenty of time.*

Longarm stifled a yawn. His desire for a cheroot was reaching the upper limits of agony.

That was one of the worse things about lurking in shadows. Frequently effective, but a man sure couldn't allow himself the pleasures of a smoke.

That would be a better reason than most for quitting the habit. But it still wasn't a good *enough* reason. And he damn sure still wanted to smoke.

He sighed. There would be time enough for that later. The only question was, how much later? He had been sitting in motionless silence now for some hours. He would be glad when his guest arrived.

Longarm amused himself for a time by recreating in his mind the pleasure Chen Li had given him, and a few more that he hoped she still would. But he had to put that out of mind as firmly as the thought of the cheroots and matches resting in his pockets. He was getting so horny he was in danger of popping his fly buttons, and it would not do for a federal officer to parade through the streets of Fairplay in that condition.

Assuming he had reason to make that little march. He checked his Ingersoll and hoped for the hundredth time that for once his assumptions might prove to be accurate.

He sighed. And waited. Patiently.

Shortly after he heard the grandfather clock strike ten, he began to believe that he had, indeed, been right. He heard what might have been the stealthy approach of footsteps outside.

Gravel, Longarm reflected, must be the bane of the burglar. That reminded him of a certain young lady not far to the north of where he now sat, but fortunately he did not have time at the moment to dwell on his regrets. He was almost sure he could hear *something* out there now.

BAALOOM!

The deep silence was shattered by the bellow of a shotgun blast, and the kitchen window buckled and fell in a cascade of glass shards.

BAALOOM! The second blast completed the job of ripping down the shade over the window, and more glass flew in a lethal spray that would have ruined a man's whole day if he had been standing in front of it.

A few feet away, beyond the pantry door, Brent MacRae's body toppled from its lifeless perch on the kitchen chair and fell with a nastily dull thump onto the

176

floor. Rigor mortis had long since set in, and the body looked unnatural in a sitting position laid onto its side.

Longarm could not help but notice that there was not a whole hell of a lot of face and upper torso left. Enough to identify the deceased, perhaps, but not a lot more. It was a good thing, he thought, that he did not have a sensitive stomach. The damage done by two loads of buckshot was about enough to gag a maggot.

Longarm had taken the liberty of borrowing a shotgun himself. He did not think that its owner, a man named MacRae, would object. And the gun should do the job, even though the heaviest shot he had been able to find in MacRae's gun cabinet had been #2. That should serve nicely at the ranges likely to be involved.

Longarm continued to sit where he was, lounging on a chair just inside MacRae's pantry.

He heard footsteps at the back door, which he had locked carefully himself before he took his seat.

Come join the party, Longarm silently welcomed his guest.

The doorknob rattled. A moment later it turned freely, and the door was pushed open.

My compliments, Longarm said to himself. *A man of many talents and a complete set of lock picks.* He smiled.

The visitor's revolver showed in the doorway first, then the man holding the gun.

He too was smiling. He walked forward to stand over Brent MacRae's shredded corpse. He nudged it with his toe, although that was hardly necessary.

Longarm grinned. "You're under arrest, Tyrone."

Broe stiffened, but did not move, although he must have been badly startled. Longarm had to give him credit for that. He was a man who had his impulses under complete control.

"I'm going to move now. Very slowly. I'm going to look at you. My hands are not going to move." They didn't, either. When he saw Longarm facing him, a cocked shotgun pointed at his middle, the bounty hunter visibly relaxed. His smile returned.

"It sure looks like I got here just ahead of you again, Deputy."

"Maybe you didn't hear me," Longarm said politely. "I said you're under arrest."

"Bullshit," Broe said with a grin.

"No, murder. I am formally placing you under arrest on the charge of the murder of Brent MacRae. If you do not surrender to me now I will, with deepest regrets, of course, be forced to take you dead rather than alive."

Broe was confused, but he was not foolish. He laid his revolver aside and placed his empty shotgun beside it. Then he backed carefully away from the guns before he said anything else.

"I'm kinda disappointed you decided to do it that way, Broe," Longarm admitted.

"Oh, I don't want no trouble with the law, Deputy." He was smiling again. "You know that. I'm a real careful man, Deputy. I never want trouble with the law."

"You'll use it and you'll abuse it, but you don't want to be afoul of it—is that it?"

"That's your interpretation, Deputy, not mine. What you don't seem to understand is that Mr. MacRae there was a wanted man. There's a five-thousand-dollar reward out for that son of a bitch back in Kansas under the name of Charles Doyle. Five thousand dollars, Long, and it's damn sure mine."

"Really? Well, that will be easy enough to prove, won't it?"

"Damn right it will." With a grin, Tyrone Broe reached out to reclaim his revolver.

For the third time in the space of a few minutes a shotgun blast roared in the MacRae kitchen, and Broe's weapons were sent skittering onto the floor.

"You really do want me to shoot you, don't you?"

Longarm said conversationally.

"I thought..."

"Now, I don't really care *what* you thought Broe. The fact is that you are my prisoner, under arrest, until or unless you prove to me that Charles Doyle is wanted for some kind of charge in the state of Kansas and that the man known here as Brent MacRae is him. You say you can do that, but first you got to show me."

"Goddammit, Long, you know as well as I do that you got a telegraph message today that—" Broe's mouth clamped shut and his eyes widened. For the first time he seemed genuinely concerned.

Longarm was the one doing the grinning now. "Telegraph message, Tyrone? I don't recall getting any telegraph message today."

"But..."

Longarm shrugged. "Not that it matters. We can check your story about MacRae, or Doyle, easily enough, with the proper authorities in Kansas."

Longarm reached under his coat to his belt and removed his handcuffs. He tossed them onto the floor in front of Broe. "You're familiar with these things, I believe. Why don't you try them on for size?"

Glaring now, and obviously worried, Broe did as he was instructed. Once the cuffs were on, Longarm laid the shotgun aside and approached him to search him. As expected, he found a hideout gun and two folding knives on him. There was also a set of spring steel lock picks which Longarm appropriated.

"Shall we take a little walk now, Tyrone?"

The bounty hunter grunted, but did as he was told.

"By the way," Longarm said in a conversational tone as he led the shackled prisoner through the streets of Fairplay, "the name could just be a coincidence, but I used to know Charles Doyle. Him and his wife were real good friends of mine. I'm just absolutely positive that

179

Brent MacRae wasn't him." Beside him Broe stumbled. "You look a little green there, Tyrone. Something you ate, maybe? A man oughta be careful about things like that."

Chapter 21

"Deputy?"

"Mmm?" Longarm laid his cheroot aside and took a soothing swallow from the glass of Maryland rye. He cocked his eye sleepily toward U. S. Marshal Billy Vail. The afternoon sunlight, he noted, was reflecting rather nicely off Billy's bald dome, but the deputy declined to mention the fact.

"You seem awfully unconcerned about the fact that the ringleader of that train robbing gang has gotten clean away."

"Oh, I don't reckon that he has," Longarm said. "Not exactly, that is. Can't prove it, of course. Not in a court of law. But there were a few things that seem to add up in that direction. A relaxation in the eyes of a man who's about to be shot down in cold blood. Names being known where they shouldn't ought to be. Little things like that. I'd say they add up a bit at a time.

"I guess I'd say that our hooded gang organizer is a fella who's made himself a secondary fortune by collecting bounty from the railroads on his own men after they've served him their purpose. And I reckon I'd say too that our smart operator with the hood and the big ideas is down in the jail right now, fixing to hang for a murder charge."

Longarm grinned. "If I had to guess, that is. Like I say, it wouldn't hold up in a court of law. But I can't get real excited about continuing the chase any further."

Longarm sat up straighter in the red leather chair he favored in Billy's office. "Which reminds me—we still have to get a warrant out for the arrest of that one boy that ran. Benny Teale, I think his name was. I can check with Tris Gay, but I think that was it."

"I thought you told me he was still in the Fairplay area."

"Now, Billy, I expect I was just wrong about that." He shook his head. "I reckon his former boss had heard that same rumor, 'cause he sure stayed around town looking for him. And then somehow was stupid enough to commit murder on an upstanding citizen of the community."

Longarm settled back in his chair and grinned. "Sure was lucky for us, eh, Billy?"

Vail tried to look angry, but did not have much success at it. "I'm still wondering about that telegram Broe claims to have seen telling you to arrest MacRae."

"The one he says you sent to me in Fairplay? Hell, Billy, I never got any such telegram. Did you send me one?"

"You know damn good and well I did not."

"Yeah? Well, there you have it. Hell, I'd lie too to keep my neck out of a noose. And he claims the *sheriff* showed him the message? That worthy official denies doing such a thing."

"Damn it, Longarm, I told you myself, not a week before this happened, that the sheriff was suspected of passing information to Broe and his partner for a cut of their profits."

"Not that I can see where one has to do with the other, Billy, but I reckon I do remember that conversation." He shook his head. "Sure don't remember getting any telegraph message about Brent MacRae, though, nor about Charles Doyle. No, sir. None of that makes any sense to me whatsoever."

Billy Vail's face was even redder than usual, but after a moment he subsided. He got up and poured some rye whiskey for both of them. "Do me a favor, Longarm."

"Sure, Billy. Anything within reason."

"Just like I can't prove anything to the courts about Tyrone Broe being the mastermind of that gang, I can't exactly prove anything about a deputy named Long being something of a conniving mastermind himself. Do you follow me so far?"

"Mmm—could be that I do."

"See that you do, Longarm. You're a good deputy, and I'd hate to lose you. But as sure as green apples make a goose shit, if you ever pull another one like this I'll have your badge in my top desk drawer before sundown. Do you follow me about *that?*"

Serious now, Longarm looked Vail straight in the eyes. "I reckon I do, Billy. I reckon I do at that."

Watch for

LONGARM IN NO MAN'S LAND

fifty-eighth in the bold
LONGARM series from Jove

coming in September!

LONGARM

Explore the exciting Old West with one of the men who made it wild!

The hottest trio
in Western history
is riding your way
in these giant
LONGARM
adventures!

The matchless lawman LONGARM teams up with the
fabulous duo Jessie and Ki of LONE STAR fame for
exciting Western tales that are not to be missed!

_____ 07386-1   LONGARM AND THE
          LONE STAR LEGEND $2.95

_____ 07085-1   LONGARM AND THE
          LONE STAR VENGEANCE $2.95